# The Trip

George Papaellinas grew up in Sydney and grew even older in Melbourne. He's been everywhere he was ever going to get and he's been nowhere yet too. His life was so much fun the first time around, he wouldn't mind another go at it all. A collection of short stories, *Ikons*, was published by Penguin Books; a novel, *No*, was published by Random House/Vintage; ABC Books published *Mumma's Kitchen*, a collection of recipes and accompanying short stories, both food for thought, compiled with Helen Addison-Smith, a great chef and writer too, the lucky duck. *The Trip* is his second novel and so far his favourite work. He has other books planned and started. He's done a lot, been in some terrific places and met some great people. He's really glad to have been alive. He'd heartily recommend it. His favourite, most memorable moment was watching the birth of his beautiful daughter, Talullah or Loula or Loulie. Helen Addison-Smith who seems able to do everything is her Mum. George has spent much of his time writing. Loulie shows him that he should have been playing more and just having fun.

## Anomaly

An anomaly deviates from a norm,
is difficult to recognize or classify.
*Anomaly* is a series which publishes
heterodox, eccentric and heretical
works. Mashing fact with fiction,
poetry with philosophy, fish with
fowl, *Anomaly* is a laboratory of
unprecedented writings.

**a re.press series**

# The Trip

## AN ODYSSEY

George Papaellinas

re.press Melbourne 2008

# re.press

PO Box 75, Seddon, 3011, Melbourne, Australia

http://www.re-press.org

© George Papaellinas & re.press 2008

The moral rights of the authors have been asserted

Database right re.press (maker)

First published 2008

*British Library Cataloguing-in-Publication Data*
A catalogue record for this book is available from the British Library

**Library of Congress Cataloguing-in-Publication Data**
A catalogue record for this book is available from the Library of Congress

*National Library of Australia Cataloguing-in-Publication Data*

Papaellinas, George, 1954-

The trip / author, George Papaellinas.

Seddon, Vic. : re.press, 2008.

ISBN: 9780980305272 (pbk)

Series: Anomaly

A823.3

Designed and Typeset by A&R
Typeset in Sabon

Printed on-demand in Australia, the United Kingdom and the United States
This book is produced sustainably using plantation timber, and printed in the destination market on demand reducing wastage and excess transport

For Loulie

# ACKNOWLEDGEMENTS

This work could not have been finished without Helen Addison-Smith and our Tallulah. I'm also very grateful to my Mum Fotini or Florence in Australia and my late Dad Constantino or Con, my sister Elena or Helen and the love in the form of writing sometimes of my beloved mates. They've all taught me so much. There's Bruce Sims who edited this work, Geoff Parish, Sharon Davis, Rosemary Creswell, Jean Bedford, Justin Clemens, Geoff Goodfellow, Brian Stagoll, Cathie Payne, Claire Thomas, Gillian Mears, the late, much-missed Sasha Soldatow, my other shockingly late mate, Jan McKemmish, the brave Bruce and the brave Helen they couldn't help leaving me behind and would've preferred not to, Catherine Murphy, Pete George, Annmarie Mauvell, Rebecca Macauley, Peter Mews, Barry Hill, Angelo and Ann Loukakis, Fiona Hile, Gus Gollings, Chloe Hooper, Jaye Kranz, Alexandra Pitsis, Mary Kalantzis, Bill Cope, Diana Kalantzis, Phil Kalantzis-Cope, Sam Brown, Ailsa Piper, Julie Davies, Alex Rizkallah, Anna Plahuta, Barbara James, Steve Dow, Patricia Cridge, Paul Demchy and Ivor Indyk.

Thank you all, you buddies.

I take full responsibility of course ... for this work alone.

*The Odyssey (sort of)*
Come on darling, tell me a story,
My muse, my goddess, my very top chick ...
Or sing it, if that's what you prefer.
Tell us the story about the tricky old guy,
The one who couldn't lie straight even in bed.
He's been in some interesting places and met some interesting people...
He's been blown around like a kite in a divine wind.
He was never going to last *forever*, not even half a god.
He was half a human too, like most people are.
He was a migrant eternally.
He just wasn't an Anglo.
He was a hero ...

*Old Odysseus*

Odysseus was an old guy who lived in the retirement village up the road from the pub.

Theo got to know him well at that pub. He recognised him later down the retirement village when the government sent him there for his Dole rolling the oldies over in their beds and hosing them down'n'out in the shower. Theo was pissed off. He'd always just expected to get his fortnightly dole cheque deposited straight into his bank account for *not* working …

Arfstraya's modget of a prime minister at the time, the terribly conservative and arguably puritanical John-John Howard couldn't just put up with him not having an official job. John-John danced to the loud and very conservative tune of Arfstrayan media commentators outraged at the very idea of old-age pensioners living off the public purse and the tune of those same old-age pensioners being even more outraged at the idea of young people getting the dole for not working and living off the public purse too. Arfstrayans put up with the Work For The Dole Scheme because they had turned as conservative as John-John. They wanted to be punished again by Daddy like naughty children. Maybe they were just being who they'd always been. I'd like to think not. But even daring to be unemployed and not being absolutely and permanently employed in the Arfstraya of once upon a time wasn't a great idea. Howard was a real modget or moral midget of a man. Jobs were made up and lied about on forms for getting the dole. Lying was officially endorsed. Arfstrayans voted for him a number of times as Prime Minister so they can't claim that they didn't know what he was on about. They obviously did.

### I'm Not Sure

I'm not sure *lived* was quite the right word to use to describe what Oddy used to do.

I'm not sure that *worked* described what Theo used to do either ...

I'm not sure that a person's having enough to eat should have to depend on whether or not they've ticked the right number of boxes on a government form just because they haven't got a job. The modget's idea wasn't a very good one, not for a democracy where everyone's at least supposed to be equal. I'm going to have to use that word *puritan* again. The modget had a theory that people had to be useful to themselves first if they were ever going to be useful to society. This was as close to a theory as John-John ever got with his Work For The Dole Scheme ...

Work and kindness were around in about equal measure in the Arfstraya of then.

### Worse Jobs

I suppose there were worse jobs around than having to listen to Oddy boring on all day, not that I care that much. I've never been all that interested in anything to do with a job. You'll be getting the whole Oddy story eventually. You'll be getting the whole Theo story first though.

I could sure use a drink when I've finished, hint, hint, hint, hint.

You do all the buying, I'll do the talking. I'll just have a drink or two while I do. I could use a drink anytime ... to tell the truth.

## Consider Yourself Lucky

Consider yourself lucky.

Most people have to go all the way to a church, fall down on their knees and talk into the sky so they can talk to god.

This is called praying. All you have to do though is just get down the local pub and find me. Most people down there wouldn't believe I'm a god, even if they had it pointed out to them a million times ... or maybe they just don't care. Maybe all they're interested in is having a beer. People down there think I'm just the old guy always slumping over a beer at the bar.

Good disguise, isn't it?

## Divine

I'm a Greek god.

That's usually called a tautology, isn't it?

I'm simply divine anyway ... and there's a whole pantheon of me living on Mt. Olympus back in old Greece. I struck out on my own and migrated to Arfstraya amongst the mortal Greek migrants. I can see where the confusion would come from.

## Half A Human

Oddy was only half an immortal god.

He was half a human too.

Telling you this is known as a revelation.

A lot of people down the pub are only half a human.

There's Mug, the owner for a start.

*I Told You*

You'll get to my story eventually like I said ...

First you'll be getting Theo's which is usually the way it is. Theo and anything to do with Theo always come first. Just ask his Mum, Mama, and all you have to do in the meantime is just shut up and listen. It's my shout, as they say.

*My Shout*

It was always my shout down the pub with Theo.

He could be what you call just a bludger. Theo wouldn't shout even if he was down the beach and a shark bit him. My drink's a beer thanks while you're up at the bar ... Theo's drink was always a Bundy'n'Coke or something fizzy and coloured.

I miss the old days sometimes, whether they were good or not. Oddy's drink used to be stiff water with a dash of scotch in it ... or a scotch-flavoured water, in other words.

*No Worries*

This story's about time.

What story isn't? First one thing happens and then another and then another and then another ... You get the story. Oddy's story is a very Arfstrayan one. It's full of winners, losers, insiders and outsiders. It's full of Arfstrayan history too. Just don't forget my divine beer, will you?

*Yesterday, Yesterday And A Bit More Yesterday*

Remember when you were just an innocent kid once upon a time?

Once upon a time is sometimes known as yesterday.

Things were always good back then. All that had to be done was playing, dancing around the living room, going wild and bacchic like some sort of drunken god, spinning and spinning around and around until you got dizzy and had to fall back into Mama's eventual arms. She would have come down to the lounge room to see just what the racket was all about. She'd hug and cuddle you all up then and all you had to do was just be.

## That's All Over Now

Well, that's all over now.

That's all in the past. It's history. All you can do now is just remember the way things used to be. Time's happened.

Remembering the past doesn't make any more difference than making up the future does. Sometimes time stops. That's known as the present ...

The present can really drag on sometimes just sitting on a bar-stool ... though I know that all time passes eventually.

I'm quite old now. I'm as old as old Methuselah, my very good mate.

## Time

There are three types of time usually called the past, the present and the future.

There are two types of people too seeing as we're counting, factory *owners* and factory *workers* who can also be called wage-slaves. There's only one kind of slave worth being though and that's a beer-slave ...

I know what I'm talking about. There's more dignity to drinking beer all day.

## Types

All people are divided into living people and dead ones.

The dead still live in a way ... I'm still living too, sort of.

Theo and Ata were living back then at least. Maybe they

still are. You *could* call Ata a friend of Theo's or a hero or something. Theo copied him a lot anyway. Ata was his god or hero or something. There were always a lot of blokes down the pub who wanted to help Ata become dead and achieve his true potential. The living can appreciate different people *because* they're different. Ata certainly always appreciated women because they weren't men. You'll hearing more about Theo and Ata soon. Ata quite liked pushing around men and hitting them. He quite liked hitting women too for all I know ... Ata and Theo had at least noticed women walking around outside in the street freely in broad daylight quite unaccompanied by any male relative. This told them they were living in Arfstraya where women walk around freely in public in broad daylight unaccompanied by a male relative. I can see how this might've been quite desirable if you were a woman though definitely not necessarily if you were an Ata or a Theo ... or a Sheik. You'll be hearing all about the Sheik soon too.

*Meeting Oddy*
I've never actually met Oddy.

It's too late now though. He's dead. I would have recognised him immediately from Theo's stories. I would've showed him every professional courtesy as one god to another. Being divine is the only logical explanation for Oddy's living so long on the planet, his *near*-immortality. He was probably just semi-divine, a demi-god or demi-mortal or something ...

*Jahweh*
Oddy wasn't the sort of god someone like Jahweh was.

No ... Oddy was real. He was just superior. He just wasn't like that boring chub Buddha was or that angry Allah guy or that old-fashioned Zoroaster one or the guy the

Aztecs worshipped with the long name or even more old-fashioned Thor or the fat Mayan guy or one of the oldest deities of all like the ones worshipped by the Bushmen of the Kalahari one or the Arfstrayan Arborigines or ones like that look like mountains or hills or rivers. Oddy was a god in the old Greek way that relies on mystery rather than miracle like the Christian heresy does ... Oddy was a god *and* a hero.

### Gods Walk
Gods are walking and flying around everywhere now.

The larger the number of gods, the larger the proof that god exists ... *if* some disbeliever out there needs something boring like proof.

### God-Bothering
Greeks have always been a great god-bothering people.

There was a god for everything in the old days. We all lived together in a house on Mt Olympus near Corinth in old Greece. We were just like other Greek families were, squabbling and fighting, loving, farting, eating, drinking too much and having to sleep it all off afterwards like in the old country.

### The Mt Olympus Milk Bar
My mortal Dad used to run the Mt Olympus Milk Bar.

It was just up the road from the beach as the holy sea's called in Arfstraya.

### Some Grand Pronouncements
People make some grand pronouncements about the past sometimes.

Or else they make some grand pronouncements ... It all just depends on your *pronounciation*.

One way or the other, things were always glorious back

then.

... People are so into the past now, it begins to sound like they're avoiding the present.

I've lived in the past and I'm telling you now that it just wasn't that hot unless it was summer outside.

Bosses and politicians just love the past ...

Things were cheaper.

## Infallible

I'm as infallible.

Gods often are.

You just have to believe everything I tell you.

I'll tell you the story of Odysseus eventually and all it will cost is a fair number of beers. OK?

## Stories And Their People

There are as many stories out there as there are people ... or kinds of people.

There's the old bloke's truth, the boy's, the woman's, the young girl's, the dog's, the cat's ... You get the idea. One story doesn't cancel out the others. You need them all if you're getting the *full* truth. You hear a lot of stories down the pub sitting on a bar-stool. A beer or two or three or four or five with a fistful of bar-nuts or chips or pretzels or something salty and tasty with your beers helps with a good story.

## Theo And Ata

The Boys were almost surprisingly not very different to each other.

The story of men and women's certainly one of the very old ones ...

Neither Theo nor Ata would've minded a woman of their own who wasn't their Mum. Their Mum *was* the number one woman in both their lives though. Living back home

10

with Mums will be the closest either of them come to living with a woman ... Neither of them knows this yet of course ... I do. I'm the god. I'm the one who can read the future.

*Me?*

I'll tell you a bit more now.

Me?

I'm still alive in an immortal sort of way. I spend my time just sitting at the bar now. The most energetic thing I do nowadays is raising my glass to my lips and sipping. I try keeping my eyes glued to the teevee behind the bar. It keeps me out of trouble. I go upstairs then where I settle down and back in my room I watch more teev on a portable, beautiful little black & white over a few more beers. I do this every night before I fall asleep. I need my life a little predictable now. I'm old ...

I mightn't be having the most exciting life in the world now. I've already had all the excitement a god can expect to have.

*Oddy?*

Oddy?

That's right. You want to know about Oddy, don't you? Well, Oddy's a well and truly dead man now ... He's well and truly a dead god too.

He used to be alive in both repects. He was alive for a mysteriously long time according to Theo. He was a jack-of-all-trades in his time. What he was used to be is called *un-skilled labour* nowadays and it's what migrants to Arfstraya mostly were.

Oddy did anything he could do for a quid once upon the time as long as it was legal ... or legal-enough.

*Forever*

You can be a migrant forever in Arfstraya if you're not an Anglo.

A lot of people think that *non-Anglo* and migrant are synonyms though they both mean something that just doesn't mean the other thing at all ...

*The End Or The Beginning Or Something*

This story's not like most stories.

It begins with the end ...

Stories more usually begin at a beginning. People *do* like to know how things end though. Beginnings and ends *are* only like bookends after all ... I might need that beer soon. Hint, hint, hint. Get one for yourself while you're up at the bar. You pay. I'll talk.

*Thanked*

Oddy never did get any thanks from a grateful nation for fighting for his country at Gallipoli.

This story's the closest thing he gets to a thank-you. It comes from a grateful me. You can show *your* gratitude just by listening. A bit of shut up and some respect don't go astray. Theo showed *his* gratitude by telling me the story he got from Oddy in the first place, the horse's mouth itself, over some foamy brown glasses foamy night after foamy night.

*The Modget And The Media*

The media just loves the modget.

What other explanation for the modget and Gallipoli and going on and on about it being on the teevee, in the newspaper and on the radio too ... The media lets him just say some really stupid things like how Gallipoli's part of Arfstraya now. It's just not. It's part of Turkey. If national borders mean anything, then Gallipoli's in another country.

Invasion and slaughter are the only way of making Gallipoli Arfstrayan. Arfstrayan Arborigines know all about invasion. The modget's just a warmonger ... You can just about pick someone who's never actually been to war themselves. They're really loud about it ... or maybe the modget just likes making noise.

### Wily And Cunning

The idea that Odysseus was a wily and cunning man just makes me laugh.

His constant smiling gave people that idea that Oddy knew what was actually going on. From what Theo told me Oddy didn't actually have a clue. That wide, spreading, chestnut grin of his was really vacant. Oddy was just an innocent witness.

### The End

This story is not like other stories.

It begins with the end.

Everything ends ... including the end. That's the end of the end or the very end ...

When Oddy came to his *very* end and died, he left his mortal coil ... or mortoil. It was probably the end of all History ...

Get it? *His* story.

### Smoke And Fire

At Oddy's very end there was lots of smoke and fire.

The only person there to wave him goodbye on his last trip was the almost entirely anonymous Stan, Stan, the Government Man as the kids in his street called him. Oddy was wearing only a cardboard box in shy, weird Stan's sweaty, shaky hands. Stan had to run around all day that day about five minutes late like a chook without a head. Stan had been up late because he'd been out the night before with all his public servant mates who were all as depressed as him. He'd stopped on the way out the door of his poky unit to check himself in one of the eighteen mirrors on his crazy walls.

He was stumbling back and dry-retching into the lonely aspidistra by the door only five minutes later. There was a lot of sun out that day thanks to Oddy's praying to his relatives, the other gods, who keep all the wet days for mortals. There was a teasing little gust of wind out that day too, a relief of a breeze on a really hot day perhaps but as it met Stan it was something of a shock. After one particularly sudden gust, Stan tripped across the brown, brown summered lawn and sent Oddy's ashes whirling up, up, up and away into the heavens where he once used to live, so not even Oddy's old bones were able to settle in Arfstraya.

## In The Beginning

When Odysseus was still young and at the other end of his life, he first found himself at sea.

He was on a ship thankfully.

The harbour front of magical Ithaca, right under the hook of Turkey's nose, was a place he liked strolling. The Oddy fairytale began there. As you know, the story ends on Arfstraya, another magical isle. In between comes most of the story of Oddy.

## Swooshing And Swaying

Oddy enjoyed swooshing and swishing on the sea before he enjoyed it as a sprog inside Mum.

Rocking and roiling came to him on a swaying deck first surrounded by boiling waves. There was a pleasing wind in his face too. Oddy started tripping. He learned everything from his Mum. First thing he learnt was taking a risk. This stood him in very good stead when he was older. She taught him to risk falling over forever by picking him up and cuddling him every time he did.

She was also the one who first taught Oddy about takeaway food way back in his Mummy's tummy. He nourished himself and just got on with being alive or whatever else he had to do. The first takeaway. When he was older and bigger he enjoyed taking away a triangle of cheese and some fruit with him whenever he went jaunting off into the forest for the day ... When he finally made it to Arfstraya, he was already enjoying solitary pleasures like eating food or getting a cuddle.

Learning how to be alone was just as well given life in Arfstraya when solitary pleasures such as gambling and running off to bookmakers to lay a bet started making really good sense eventually. Other people can only interfere with *solitary* pleasures ...

Oddy became a huge five-cent punter when he was a much older child in the retirement village. He just needed his own telephone. If Oddy couldn't lay a big bet then, he'd lay a small one. Gambling made him feel warm and secure like being kissed and cuddled by his Mum. His mind was quite addled then but Oddy always had enough wits for laying bets. Oddy would have even bet on which fly would get to the top of a wall first in the retirement village.

*At The End Of The Trip*
At the end of his long trip, Oddy enjoyed being fed regularly and coddled again like when he was still a bub. Every wish was like a command then too. He was a little guy again when he was an old guy too and he shrank and became the captain of his last ship. It was a huge, white, billowing ocean of a ship. The nurses at his retirement home called it a bed.

He only had to buzz and buzz and buzz for a nurse passing by like a ship in the night for a well-blended liquid meal or a hospital cup of tea with frozen, long-life milk and seven sugars and a plastic straw bending in the middle so he could enjoy it over a sweet or sour junket for breakfast, lunch and dinner.

All his nurses were sort of in love with Oddy like ladies had been all his long life.

Disembarking forever eventually came as a surprise to him ... There was smile of pure bliss on his lips. Oddy loved his last minutes in Arfstraya too.

## Blaming Mama

Blaming Mama for everything that ever went wrong in your life has always been fashionable.

Oddy's Mama couldn't have cared less if he blamed her for anything or not though. She was dead.

She was living in Hades instead of on the surface of the planet. She'd grown quite used to being blamed for everything that ever went wrong by Oddy's *mortal* Dad, the freedom-fighting, guerilla pirate dolt the Ottoman Turks captured and roasted alive on a spit over a slow fire when she was still married to him. This *was* the closest Antikleia or Anti, Oddy's Mum, ever came to getting any attention from him. The first man in her life, Daddy, made her hubby look kind in comparison. All the men in Anti's life back on Ithaca were a disappointment ... except for her little boy, Odysseus when he was just a kiddy god who just adored her. He even followed her off Ithaca when she left the place ... which literally became god-forsaken when Oddy left. He just wasn't the bastard some people down the pub called him behind his back sometimes. His Mum and his mortal Dad were married secretly in a very secret Greek Orthodox Christian church in Ottoman, Muslim Greece.

## Mummy-tummy

Oddy's mummy decided it might be best if Oddy's Dada didn't know Oddy was on the way.

He might piss off if he did so Oddy just had to keep as quiet as he could. He only made quiet bubby sounds, putt-putt-putt, gurgle-gurgle-gurgle and all the usual noises one makes inside one's Mum.

Secret swimming hadn't finished yet for Oddy. His first swim was a secret one. It was in a secret baptismal font in a secret church in a secret cave ... or splish-splash as Oddy called it at the time.

## Religion

The *two* equally true faiths of the time collided with each other in that corner of the world.

I'm talking all about Islam and Christianity. As religions they were almost as big as football is in Arfstraya ... of whatever code. *Muslim* vs *Infidel* was the name of the biggest game ... All it's just superstitious nonsense though, if you ask me ... and I know very well what I'm talking about. I play another game altogether, the *really* true faith one.

## Ma and Pa

Oddy's Mum was just an innocent girl in a world full of horny pirates like Oddy's Dad.

Dad just saw her as plunder, as booty as well as booté. She was just another notch on his cutlass or scratch of a quill on his pirate's map or whatever ...

Oddy's Mum and Dad never did live happily ever after, not least because Oddy's Dad didn't get to live much longer at all. He was soon just another revolutionary kebab. Oddy's Mum barely noticed when he disappeared for the last time. He often did ... if only for the weekend.

She just wasn't sure though. He was often disappearing

up his mountain to be with his mates. He'd always been a lousy companion for a young girl to be saddled with.

*Mind You*

Mind you, the absent husband and father was an old island tradition.

War, migration and fleedom ... or freedom rather were traditions on the island.

Oddy was proof of the fact that his Daddy came down from his mountain for split minutes at a time or long enough at least to vent some spleen and yell at her a bit before having his way with his Mum just in case before looking in on his mens' lonely guerilla wives.

Leaving pirate wives at home to take responsibility for domestic drudgery like the cooking, the cleaning, the weaving and sewing and looking after the children and other domestic animals was what just everybody just had to do. This was seen as the best way of keeping pirate wives from getting bored and lonely. The difference between a pirate wife and a pirate widow wasn't always clear in those dark days of the past. Men risked dying in the seemingly endless fighting with Turks in the name of liberty and equality and other fancy French revolutionary notions current at the time. Revolutionary fervour born of the French Revolution and the guillotine for all oppressive aristocrats and other rulers was flaming the whole world back then ... almost. The blacks in Arfstraya continued just being black and oppressed. Whites imagined that revolutionary fervour was only something they could do.

Sororité rather than fraternité was never a huge catch-cry up the mountain amongst the hairy, sweaty fellers there. Island wives weren't particularly encouraged to stand shoulder to shoulder with their men against a common oppressor.

The next generation of subjects had to be looked after and brought up by somebody. The blokes had to do all the fighting to the strains of *bouzoukia* blaring the national anthem ... or the national something, the little girls had to ... do something.

## Hasty

Oddy's Mama got a reputation for being hasty sometimes.

She thought that she was really in love with Oddy's Dad ... Love's often mixed up with lust ... Oddy's Daddy had heard all about pretty Anti from his men and just wandered down the mountain to check her out for himself. Boys in those days quite liked a good gossip ... One consequence was that Oddy's Mum had to get married in a hurry then. Oddy was already on the way. Life under her husband's roof after the first flush of passion had flushed wasn't that different to life under brutish Daddy's. The first flush of passion because of Oddy's Dad turned out to be her last flush with him. Oddy's Mum quite liked a good flush too even though she was recently only an inexperienced girl who just got sweet-talked by Oddy's swashbuckling, sweet-talking Daddy ... before he got cooked. The community back then would've punished her rather than rooty Dad if they hadn't been married when they ... embraced. People lived much more by the community's rules back then.

## Hillbillies

Oddy's grand-people were hillbillies.

There weren't hills on the island though.

There *was* a big mountain though so Oddy's people could be called mountain-billies. They were old-fashioned farming and fishing folk or peasants anyway.

There were always some things best done at night back then too or by the un-shine of a cloudy moon and that was when Oddy's Dad liked looking in on his men's lonely wives too and transacting all his other transactions like Turk-killing and loving was important too.

The lack of any present or future stuck on lonely Ithaca and the daily hard groan of work in her cruel Daddy's olive groves and vineyards meant that Oddy's Mum was just about panting to get away. She was a comely wench too who was hoping for just a kind word or two from Oddy's Dada well as that ... flushing. Her major problem was that she didn't just have a great body. She had a great brain too.

*Handsome Dad*

Handsome Dad just didn't want to die in a heathen cause as an infidel conscript rather than shooting Turkish overlords or cutting latté-coloured Turkish throats rather than in the service of Jeebut or Jeezels or whatever his Christian god was called.

When her flush had flushed and reason had taken over, Oddy's Mum decided that she'd had quite enough of his uncouth Dad, even if he wasn't that bad a result given the average age of his competition on the island even if he turned out to be ridiculously fast in the you-know-what department she ever came across. Luckily for most fellers there have always been other considerations too. He did have a curly-haired bellows for instance ... and other considerations too.

*Quite Revolutionary Or Quite Revolting*

It's hard to know whether Oddy's Dadda was only a *revolutionary* or just *revolting*.

There's not much point asking Oddy's Mum. We already know what she thought. She just wasn't much of an island wife. She had far too many ideas of her own.

Some no doubt well-intended teacher thought he was doing her a favour when he taught her how to read by the oily light of a lamp at night. Anti never settled down into a life as a decent Ithacan village wife just waiting for husband to come home from his freedom-fighting or his voyaging or his emigrating. She wasn't the type to just take up weaving or sewing for some company once the kids had grown up and left home.

### Pregnant

Anti could get pregnant just going for a stroll next a bloke.

She liked ... *strolling.*

An island community with its thousand eyes was no place for a woman like Antikleia.

She left the island for Arfstraya as soon as she could, like many Ithacans already had and many more would one day ...

The island's wine has always been legendary and legend has it that Antikleia didn't mind the odd glass of the local grape. An unearthly light lit the Ithacan sky one night. It wasn't just the grog though that often got Anti's hand up her dress. This light seemed to be helping her hand go further up her dress than it had ever gone before. Soon Anti was glow-glow-glowing and after-glowing. She just had to swoon.

This obviously wasn't just a visit from another nervous, mortal hill-fighting fan of her husband's. Whoever this was knew what he was doing. Oddy's real Dad was clearly a god, a Big Daddy. That has to surely be the explanation for why Odysseus lived so long. He was nearly an immortal, a Big Daddy. Odysseus was obviously an *almost*-eternal being.

### Up The Mountain

Oddy's mortal Daddy eventually took his boy up the mountain with him once Mum had house-trained him properly. He wanted to show his boy off to his hill-fighting comrades. He just forgot to tell Oddy's Mum.

Up a mountain was a very boring place for a young tacker ...

Oddy's Dad found things he had to do that were much more important than looking after his own flesh and blood almost as soon as they got up there. He was just pursuing another old island tradition. At first he just left Oddy in the chilly guerilla stores cave on his well-padded, well-nappied increasingly smelly behind where he decided that little Oddy could be safe there as long as he didn't play with any knives, swords or loaded pistols there. His divine relatives leaned over their cloud from up high or whatever, wherever, and kept a blesséd eye or two on him.

Oddy was already Oddy. He'd got busy sorting the guerilla weapons into useful piles. He labelled the pile of broken goods that could still be repaired GO AND GET. He labelled one of things that were beyond repair STUFFED.

The thought came to his Dad eventually that the baby might catch cold so his Dad tucked him under a burly arm and stowed him in the warmer guerilla kitchen on a pile of dead fish there waiting to be cleaned and simmered slowly in a tomato and vegetable ragout for guerilla dinner.

That was where the Oddy legend has it that he slept with the fishes ... He'd do this again one day out the back of his latest takeaway fried fish, chip, saveloy and dim-sim shop in Arfstraya a whole ocean and age away when he was older ... His all-too busy hillfighter Dad got sick of him and shoved him under that burly arm again and took him back down the mountain and handed him back to his Mum who had become hysterical by now and just wanted him back ...

*Happy Kid*

Oddy was outside in the sun a lot.

All the happiest kids are found there, his sharp-eyed

Mum kneeling over her little patch of garden. She parked him out of the way on the concrete around the bottom of the hills-hoist, an early Greek invention, while she got on with her sweeping, her bed-making, her filo pastry-rolling, her sewing, her weaving and anything else around the house that popped up. His Mum had always stayed a peasant lass, turning soil and watching things grow. The worst thing Oddy ever copped from her was a smile.

Her Oddy was never too much trouble. In summer she even dragged his wading pool outside for him to paddle in the sun in. This was quite an effort too. Wading pools were carved out of stone back then. Oddy hadn't grown up yet and invented plastic.

## Eyes, Eyes And More Eyes

Little Oddy found the bushes all around him in the back-yard full of eyes, eyes, eyes and eyes.

They belonged to the bunny rabbits hopping all over the island. Oddy eventually chose the humble bunny to represent him as his good-luck totem.

You can just imagine how Oddy felt when he came to Arfstraya and learnt that the place was full of hasty millions of them … He just knew then that he'd come to the right place to live.

## Styx And Stones

I'm a god.

I can do whatever I want to. I know we've just done at the beginning of Oddy. We're jumping to the end of Oddy now, to when he died and crossed the River Styx into Hades. He could begin enjoying his after-life … for eternity then.

Oddy was Oddy the shade now.

He'd run out of choices and having a choice about things is one of those things that defines someone as still alive.

*Turning Your Back*

When people migrate, they often turn their back forever on everything they know.

They're hoping they can start exercising a choice about things again.

By the time Oddy got to the Styx, bumbling along in death much as he always had in life, slowed down only by all the other deadheads bumping into him along the way. When Oddy's shade, ex-Oddy, got to the river, it found that Charon, the ferryman had zipped off for a sit-down somewhere that *wasn't* a boat.

Charon pockets the coins family or friends screw into an ex-person's sightless eyes to cover the fare. Ex-Oddy didn't have the fare though. You need friends or family so it was lucky in fact that Charon wasn't there. Oddy's shade, Not-Oddy Anymore, waited a while, got bored and decided to get to the other side by swimming. Even dead Arssies love a swim and Oddy had always wanted to be any sort of Arssie so he swam and became a glade or glad shade.

*Only Water*

The Styx was only water ...

Oddy the glade shucked its ghostly clothes. Being already dead, Odysseus no longer had to hold his breath. He took an unearthly, deep breath and swam underwater across to the other side where he saw his entire future as a dead man laid out ... It just *wasn't*. His mate from the very old days, old Achilles turned up then and hailed him.

'O brave Odysseus,' began the over-aged hero.

'Welcome to nothingness forever where even the life of the most humble takeaway food man from Arfstraya is preferable ... '

'It's not too bad here,' fibbed ex-Oddy bravely, struggling

with the truth. Then thankfully, Achilles' once-handsome decayed face stopped trying to crack a lop-sided grin. Oddy would've probably preferred not to be dead.

## Hades

Hades is just *not*.

A person does *not* have a mortal body there or mortal coil or mortoil anymore. Everyone's always smiling insincerely there. It's really creepy. There's no grinning. That would be too energetic. There's no kissing, no cuddling, no making love, no making hate or making anything. It's not Heaven, it's not Hell, it is just Hades. No one ever goes hungry there though, not like in some living, mortal places ...

## The Last Resort

You know why I'm changing the subject this time?

I'm changing the subject again this time just because I feel like it ...

I wish I could just do whatever I feel like whenever I feel like it because I feel like seeing Ithaca again. There's a beautiful front beach there.

Have you ever been in really high summer?

Oddy has.

He migrated to somewhere nicer eventually ... to even nicer Arfstraya. Naked, brown shoulders blister beautifully in the blessed sun there too. This reminds of what things used to be like when Oddy was just a boy on Ithaca and still had shoulders. His Mum would always be waiting for him there with a cool glass of cooling water for him. Cool waves crash on and on at the beach there. It feels beautiful there, it sounds beautiful, it is just beautiful ... Oddy could never have forgotten the place if he'd lived there even longer ... or lived even longer anywhere at all.

*Penelope*

That was Penny the nurse sitting next to him at Oddy's last bed and holding his hand when he needed it.

People like company when they're dying ... Gods do too.

Oddy was beginning to breathe very shallowly and Penny knew just what this meant.

She didn't just sit there because it was her job and she had to or anything. She actually, *really* liked him. I think that Oddy might've been weaving his old magic and using his charm even at the end. Ladies were always waiting on Oddy. Penelope sat up all night next to him, her needle in one hand and her tapestry frame with a tapestry in it in the other. It's hard to know what Penny was better at, sewing or waiting for a bloke ...

*Fluttering Eyelids*

Oddy's eyelids fluttered every now and then just to keep Penny awake.

Describing him as alive would almost be an exaggeration though. He didn't drive Penny any madder than any other dying old coot on the ward copping a sneaky feel at her expense here and another there did. Maybe Oddy charmed her too. He was always doing that with ladies.

She'd decided earlier that she could relax with her looming and weaving when she got home. She'd almost been fantasising about her loom all day at work, loom-less hour after loom-less hour ... She'd weave each night until bed-time every night and then she'd even weave some more in bed and then weave herself to sleep.

Whenever she overcame her shyness for long enough to speak to one of the other nurses, she talked weaving. Weaving was never not on her lips even on the phone on the rare occasion she rang someone. She even described life itself as just like weaving, full of the fundamental weave and weft of things ...

Penny didn't suffer a shortage of suitors when she was older. They were all interested in her assets. They were all interested in her money, I mean, rather than in any of her ... more personal assets. She'd saved quite a lot of money. Penny didn't really have a lot to spend her money on. Her wages just added up and went straight into her bank account, electronically. The modern world is just full of mysteries *and* miracles.

Anyway. Penny leaf-leaf-leafed through one of those endless woman's magazines of hers as she sat next to Oddy's bed to while away some time. It was something to do. She was enjoying herself as much sitting next to Oddy's bed as she enjoyed herself when she just sat thoughtlessly at home leaf-leaf-leafing through an endless woman's magazine in her mostly empty house. While she waited, waited and waited, Oddy's speckled, bald old head was poking out from under his balding chenille bedspread, a top sheet tucked in tight around his flappy old throat. Oddy slept as deeply as he used to when was a kiddy. He was rattle-rattle-rattling like some sort of baby's toy winding down. He was dreaming a very last dream at the end of his very long, dreamy trip of a life. Penny should've been paying more attention. What the rattling Oddy was doing was probably something like the wisdom of the ages and the very meaning of life itself.

*Horseys*

Oddy was dreaming about horses.

He'd been following and betting on horses ever since he arrived in Arfstraya a long time ago. He even dream-dreamt about horses in his very last bed in hospital. He'd always enjoyed a flutter on the gee-gees ... at the races. Playing the odds and laying bets had been one of his greatest pleasures for a long time now. Oddy had always earned much income like this. All too often though the horses Oddy lost so much money on weren't even horses. They were bloody donkeys ... Oddy would've bet on a racing bunny hopping in a rabbit-race if there was nothing else to bet on. One of the horses in tired, old Oddy's floating life of dreams that very last night of his was a brown, old, blinkered workhorse, a real nag, as depressed and depressing as old Oddy himself, always waiting and waiting patiently where it was parked on the street Oddy always trotted down on the way to his *kafeneion* in the city. This nag was always tethered to a tourist coach there, as polished and shiny as the dusty, old nag just wasn't. It was always there for just anyone to look at. The old workhorse didn't even have a privacy it could call its own at the end of another long day's plodding, one bag for catching poo strapped to its bum like a nappy and another bag full of oats or pre-poo strapped to its other end. This persistent old dream horse of Oddy's chew-chew-chewed and cudded through its last days ...

'Ratta-tatta-tatta-tatta-tatta-tatta-tatta-tatta-tatta-tatt,' went Oddy just then bringing Penny's head up.

### The One Very Last Breath

Oddy didn't breathe just *one* last breath.

He'd been breathing a whole series of last breaths for ages. His every breath was a last breath. It was otherwise called his life. The first last breath he took was when he was born and copped his first smack on the bum. A tiny, little baby's rattle came soon after that thankfully.

### Oddy Becomes History

Oddy exited his life in much the same way as he came in.

He didn't have much of a clue. Oddy became history himself.

## Hats Off

Take your hands out of your pockets.

Take your hat off too and join me in drinking a toast to good old Oddy ... or just join me in having a drink.

## The Full Oddy Story

Oddy's life was a long series of moments.

I'll tell you some of them soon.

There were horses in many of them. I've already mentioned that old nag on the street. Another of Oddy's dream horses stood out in Theo's memory too. It was a real nightmare of a black, black horse apparently. Oddy shuddered as he told Theo about it apparently.

Oddy was still a sort of young man apparently tom-catting his way around town when he came across this horse ... or vice versa. The streets in those days were stone and loud. Oddy's hair was black and wavy under his snappy hat. Oddy wore a smart, blended wool suit with a fine brown pinstripe too. The night was a deepest, blackest blue. An almighty clatter clattered behind him. Oddy turned on dreamy heels. He was always too late. A shiny, very black carriage drawn by two mad, wild-eyed black horses was glaring down on him. Oddy's heart raced like it was going to burst. He froze. This might've been Oddy's darkest dream.

## Last Night

Last night was a huge one.

It was a real dinosaur of a night. I might've downed me one or two beers too many and passed out eventually on my bed up the stairs down the pub. I had to get me up a lot through the night to get to the toilet. The old waterworks were going mad ... I was always just in time. The light coming through my window kept waking me up. The sun was telling me what time of day it was. Morning was white.

Black meant night.

Theo was buying the beers the night before for once.

### The Orange Vinyl Curtain

I brought my orange vinyl down on my head by mistake this morning. My blind was giving me the shits and I wanted it out of the way so I probably pulled it too quickly. I blame all the beer Theo bought last night as we cacked and yacked. I had my usual Frosty Bran for breakfast. There was still some milk left in the fridge. I had my usual couple of googies on toast too with my usual couple of palate-cleansing ales. I barely got a glance at the morning newspaper. It was full of old bones or the discovery of them rather. A pile of old Arfstrayan dinosaur bones had been found. They were Arfstrayan dinosaur bones so they were the very oldest naturally. They were marsupial bones too so they were very Arfstrayan in fact. The pile included the bones of *Procoptodon Goliath*, a whopper kangaroo who I once knew by its real name, Hoppy. The pile included the bones of *Phascolonus Gigas* or Cuddles, the big, carnivorous wombat ... If it's possible to imagine a platypus, then I reckon it's possible to imagine anything. Arfstrayan mega-fauna have always been the biggest. There's a Giant Prawn, a Giant Trout and a Giant Sheep too close to its Giant Sheep Dog sitting on the giant tucker-box outside Tips-Me-Hat, a couple of hundred kilometres inland from Surfing on the coast.

### Archaeopteryx

Not all Arfstrayan dinosaurs were the biggest.

Some of them were the smallest.

That pile of bones included the skeleton of a Compsognathus, a tiny bird-like creature as light as a feather. The bones of the famous Archaeopteryx were in that pile too. These were thought in the past to be a hoax. A hoax is a very Arfstrayan thing, like any sort of joke. I think I saw an Archaeopteryx once though. I'm just not sure though. Gods are just like people in one respect at least. They see whatever they want to see ...

## Yokel
Most people saw Theo only as a yokel, a dummy or idiot ...

They weren't always wrong ... Theo wasn't any more stupid than some of the other people down the pub who had big, important jobs though ...

## Something Almost Happens
Theo liked sleeping in of a morning after a night before.

Mama didn't really approve but she really had no say. He'd been up all night before down the pub with his mates or on a corner somewhere with them. I was there too for the pub part of his evening and I can tell you Theo drank a fair bit. He was matching me drink for drink. He couldn't see why he should have to get up just because his Mum got up early to clean their flat.

She just wouldn't let poor Theo sleep. She kept running the loud vacuum cleaner back and forth, back and forth on the loud parquetry floor just outside his bedroom door. He groaned loudly at her to shut up, go away and go away. He had a bad headache from all the beer the night before. There was just no point being unhappy about him sprawling in this morning, all tangled up in his sheets and in his dreams. She knew that he'd just got to bed. Theo's Dad had also liked sleeping in, Mama reminded herself ... She reminded herself that all men did too. She tried explaining to him that she wasn't his slave but she made him a late breakfast anyway. She prepared some slices of fresh tomato from the garden for him and she spooned some creamy sheep's yoghurt onto his plate from the sheep ... from the shop, I mean. She sprinkled fresh oregano from the pot plant on the kitchen over some tiny black olives in olive oil on his plate. She also got some yummy heated, sesame-dusted crescents of bread out of the oven.

Theo's Mama was as black in her widow's shroud and tiny as one of her olives. She had a groaning look to her. Theo's Mama told herself to hold her tongue until he'd had his shower at least but she finally just had to raise her voice at him. Every morning would groan on like this and finally Mama would start crying and apologise and apologise at him for not letting him sleep in longer *again* until he was almost crying ...

*Gangling*

Theo ignored Mama for as long as he could but he got up in the end, pushed his plate away and gangled his way down the main drag as quickly as he could in his usual slow-going, stoned way. Theo even dressed down and slowed his way into his future dressed just the way he wanted to. He actually thought he looked sharp in his baggy American jeans and sloppy, loose T-shirt. The only places he ever went were quite close to where he lived thankfully because Theo didn't actually like having to make an effort. He'd go to the Dole Shop, the pub and to the local disco that were all close by. He'd gangle to them all as slowly as he wanted to as slow as the syrup dripping down one of his Mama's *baklavathes*.

He always got to the Dole Shop in time which was the only place he had to keep to a clock for. The place's desk-jockeys would all be lolling outside against a wall catching rays with ciggies hanging out their mouths before they had to interview clients like Theo and give him some boss in a smart tie who'd demand a full day's work from Theo whose slownesss was a kind of very Arfstrayan two-fingered salute and up-you to society ... He blew one of his juicy, big fat after-breakfast joints as he gangled along listening to the laughter raining down from the heavens that only he could hear. He was wearing a loose number thirteen, green'n'gold gridiron top.

## Bright Sparks

Theo wasn't the only bright spark around those parts.

All the Boys he grew up with were as sparky as he was. They all wore low-crotch baggy jeans from The States. They were all Arfstrayans, the Lebos, the Grecos, the Eyeties, the Skippies, all of them. They were one big bag of mixed lollies, brothers all with their own anthem from that song from the movie about street-gangs, West Side something, the *when you're a Boy, you're a Boy from your first big fat joint to your last dying day* song or however it goes.

Theo's Mum ironed her love right into his jeans every morning, creasing deep lines up or down both legs with her iron even though he'd asked her not to about a million times. Theo so didn't like looking like a dag or retard. He just wanted to look sharp instead in his American jeans or in his tracky dacks ... He sometimes wondered whether Mama just ignored him and ironed them like that on purpose just to embarrass him in front of his Boys. Whatever he wore though, *he* was the one wearing it so they looked pretty cool ... The Dole Shop had sent him down the old folks' home and he just had to get down there today, if he wanted any Dole that fortnight, that is.

## Evil

There was evil living down the Dole Shop according to Theo.

It wore a grey cardigan and an earring in just one ear if it was a man and another in just one nostril and another in one lip. If it was a woman, it wore a floral, A-line cotton frock. Theo attended some compulsory visits to the Dole Shop for stern discussions about his future. When he got there he'd sit on his balled fists in the waiting area or cattle-yard as it was also known. The fortnightly pittance he got was only good for a few packets of cigarettes.

## One Earring

All the other Boys wore just one earring in one ear too.

Theo didn't like looking *too* different ... and if anyone down the street saw them wearing their earring and called them a poofter or something, The Boys would circle them and give them a good kicking. *One for all and all for one* or something original like that was the motto the gang adopted as its own. Theo would get out of the Dole Shop as quickly as he could and go find his mates up the road so he could hang out with them on a corner all night.

The Dole was quite a cheap way for the Government to deal with shiftless unemployed young people like Theo who it could get to do anything at all and that person just had no choice about it if they didn't want to lose the Dole. Slavery was back ... Someone waiting down the Dole Shop told Theo all about the good old days once upon a time before the modget and his Work For The Dole thing happened and Arfstraya started becoming a mean place. Work For The Dole even sounded like a government scam ... I mean government scheme. Who says that you can't fool all of the people all of the time?

## The Old Folks' Home

The Dole Shop sent Theo to the old folks' home for a fort-night.

Getting him used to holding a job was the official explanation so it was the Dole Shop brought Theo and Oddy together. Theo had to learn something useful like how to wash bedpans for nothing. It was a job though ... and the future the modget was busy designing was supposed to be a bright one.

Theo hummed a song he'd heard somewhere as he dragged his heels towards the old people's home. The words to the tune he hummed were something like *a man's just gotta do what a man's gotta do.* Who knows from where it came. His new sort-of job was something at least or so Mama thought. Theo wasn't great at rattling the establishment.

### Down, Down, Down The Road

At least her Theo was getting somewhere, even if it was just up or down the road in tracksuit pants thought Mama.

Theo was a big boy. Some people would have even called him fat. Theo wasn't gangling. He was waddling. The Boys were all on the bigger side. So were the girls. Theo looked forward to being a big man around where he lived one day when he was older. He wanted a flunky of his own one day too, someone even flunkier than he was now.

### The Future

Theo could see the future sometimes if he shut his eyes.

The future wasn't going to be all that different from the present or the past.

There was a wall just down the road from the pub pasted with posters featuring loud, garish letters that were peeling off it like some sort of dead skin. All their words were set in the future but the events they advertised were already over. Time was messy even then. One of the loudest posters advertised a kick-boxing match promoted by the company Theo fantasised about working for one day. He also fantasised that his best mates, the other Boys, worked there too. His fantasy was a very cosy one indeed. Theo imagined putting his own big bucks that he made selling smack at the blood-sports his company would be promoting. Fighting had always been popular around where Theo lived. The biggest matches would work by exploiting old ethnic rivalries like Turks vs Greeks or Greeks vs Macedonians or something ethnic and versus. The company would make a fortune and it had a name already even which was something like *Arfstraya Inc.* Theo wanted to be a hero around his old streets one day and wanted to become even richer than in his folks' wildest dreams.

Theo talked to me a lot over drinks about his big ideas for making money through his company one day. Theo's head was always working on schemes for making money. It might have been the only part of him that worked. Theo had worked out an idea for a Talent Quest, the Miss Loukoumi Quest and he was hoping to work on a sponsorship deal worth some really big bucks from Loukoumi Inc. which was his uncle on his Mum's side who was making a fortune in the confectionary and other sweet things such as sugar cubes business.

Old Money has always used family connections. Old Boy networks and Old School Tie networks have always been important. Theo relied on *New* Boys' networks and *New* Money. There was lots of money in moving white powder or rock or product or whatever it'll be called then which won't be a dirtier business than places where Old Money comes from.

*Laundry*
Theo has even worked out how to launder the huge profits from his promotion company.

Theo's Mum took in other peoples' washing for money once upon a time ... Laundering was obviously like a family tradition.

Theo had obviously thought about it a bit and decided he could use the books from the dance-music clubs he also imagined he'd run and be promoting through his company. He mentioned ... phat, phat, fully sick flavour men ... whatever that meant. I think that maybe *promoting* is just another way of saying *telling* someone and apparently *flavour men* meant DJs or something. He told me that some time later on. These ... *flavour men* ... would all have strange names like Dope Killer, Kunning Kuts and Kid Hero.

Theo was a strange enough name in Arfstraya once upon a time.

### Lost

Theo will be so lost in his own thoughts one day that he'll just ignore a scream from down the road ... and step in front of the stream of cars.

That's how he'll be killing himself one day and it just won't be possible to know whether he actually meant to or not. This applied to just everything of course. It wasn't ever possible to know what was just an accident and what wasn't.

### The Day Of Mama

Anyway.

Theo crept slowly by the old Halal Butcher down his main drag the day he pushed off from the table where he lived with Mama. Its front window was always full and full of trays and trays of dead. It sat next to a jeweller's with trays and trays of gold and silver crucifixes or crescents that he might or might not have stolen the night before when he Theo had probably seen them all before when he broke and entered other people's homes with one of the other Boys and took them to one of the hockshops on the street for only a fraction of their actual worth ... Next door to one of the pawnbrokers up the road sat a cake shop or *zacharoplasteion* with a window full of trays and trays of dusty sugar treats soaked in syrup and covered in crushed nuts just like Mama made.

He stopped in front of the pooch palace next door too and watched the playful puppies scrambling all over each other until one of them could make it to the top of the heap in the dog-eat-dog world they lived in. There was a Chinese milkbar next door too that would sell overpriced smokes under the counter with a wink-wink-wink to under-age anyone with the money. Theo knew his main drag so well that he could float down it stoned and switched right off just musing to himself like the stoner that he was on his slow way to the old folks' home where whatever was going to be was just going to be.

*Theo Mused A Lot*
Theo liked musing like I say.
The streets always belonged to the likes of Theo and his Boys. There was an inside and outside in the mortal world back then too.

*Jobs*
Theo couldn't very well put breaking and entering or smack-dealing down as jobs on his Dole form to get the Dole as if he was just another member of society ... which I suppose he was. The Dole was the right of everyone who needed it rather than just *wanted* it, whatever the difference was. It would've been nice if Theo could just do his own thing rather than work at any of the bullshit slave-labour jobs the Dole Shop sent him to ...

## Ata's Corner

Theo became so lost in thought that he got to Ata's corner without getting nervous.

Ata was one of the big cheeses around here and frightened Theo too ... Little Theo was just fifteen and he didn't want his life to ever change ... He paused on his snail-trail up the road. Something *had* changed. A woman's clothes shop painted bright pink was where something else used to be once. Theo couldn't remember exactly what ... Something tried and true. The dope was having its way with Theo, I think.

'That's right.' Theo finally remembered. It came to him at last. There used to be a hot and cold takeaway food shop there. Theo could remember it very well in fact. The *tzatziki* on the kebabs was as light as clouds. It was as tasty as kissing ... Loud music was pouring out of the dress-shop down Theo's street.

## Hip-Hop Crap

'Hip-hop crap,' thought Theo to himself in a pooh-poohing sort of way.

He preferred good old-fashioned, wall-shaking rock'n'roll.

He'd often turn the jukebox in the old takeaway right up and listen. Theo's main street thundered with cars.

The music from the new pink palace just added to the noisy mess already there. It smelled of flowers or perfume or incense or something too. Theo turned his nose up at it or because of it or something it.

## Richie Riches

Theo's whole world was changing.

His main drag was just the beginning.

Richie Riches were taking over.

Theo had even begun shaping up for a fight. He'd already lost though.

He decided that he'd become rich himself one day and move to where *they* came from. He'd get his own back one day in that way.

## Not Too Shabby

Theo was checking himself out in passing windows like a poofter.

'Not too shabby,' Theo told himself, sucking in his big, fat, sucking tummy.

He wore his long dark hair oiled back and black like Ata did too. He shaved the back of his neck every morning too.

Theo was so waxed and polished he shone. He wore some gold bracelet too and a shiny chain around his thick neck and his smartest tracky dacks too under a big, loose T-shirt. He could imagine the pale, hippy-hoppy chicks checking him out.

## Chicks Are Such Chicks

Theo had dealt with all girls the same way for a long time now.

'Chicks are such chicks,' he told me once down the pub.

'Bloody women!'

He wondered whether maybe he needed to be spending even more time down the gym and smoking less dope and far fewer cigarettes so he could get even fitter. He was getting sick of chicks looking through him and pretending that he wasn't even there.

Maybe he was just too much man for the skinny, white Arfstrayan, hippity-hoppity scrags. Maybe he was too macho or mucho or something ...

These chicks obviously weren't virgins like his sister.

## Attaboy Cornered

Attaboy never changed.

Possibly because he was just too perfect the way he was.

Ata mostly hung out on the corner near the kitchenware place with the shiny, shiny handmade, authentically ethnic cooking-pots hanging outside on hooks ...

Ata stood on that corner, *his* corner. His legs looked sculpted in the tight, elastic jeans he liked wearing, a tight T-shirt with them that barely covered his curly, bursting bush of chest and looked tighter than anything Theo ever fitted into. Ata was Theo's hero. He wore thicker rolled gold chains around his neck than Theo did. Theo tried not to stare at Ata in case Ata thought he was a homo who couldn't tear his eyes off him. Ata reminded himself to bash Theo one day soon just in case *he* was the poofter. Attaboy didn't even twitch a cheek as Theo rounded the corner ... Ata grew up in Turkey where poppies turn whole acres into a blanket of red. Ata liked the pinballs in the takeaway where he hung out and attracted the attention of the local cops because he'd started charging protection money. The local shopkeepers all paid happily or so they all told him. Someone had to pay for Ata. Local heroes don't just come for nothing.

## The Sheik

The Sheik was another local hero of Theo's.

Jesus once died to wash away Theo's sins his Mama kept reminding him. She did worry a bit about her boy's Sheik-ing but the truth was that she only half-minded. The Sheik was at least a good religious man even if he was Turkish Muslim and a fanatic one. He was a wog at least and not an Arfstrayan or a skip. She didn't really worry about The Boys or Ata either. At least The Sheik stopped The Boys killing each other or shouting at women just trying to pass by in the street. The Sheik actually hated women for being so unclean but this didn't really matter. The Sheik needed an army and The Boys needed a General so everyone was happy. The Greeks and Turks are just like each other. She only half-worried about Theo going out all night too. At least he was getting out of the house and getting some fresh air. She did wish that he'd do it more through the day while she was cooking or cleaning or doing something around the house and actually needed him out of the way. Theo was a man after all just like his father was before he died and went to heaven of course and became another angel.

*Ata Stories*

Theo heard at least eighteen Ata stories around the traps.

Theo was a real Ata fan.

That many stories make a legend or a myth ... Theo could repeat every word of every story. Some of the stories were so tall Theo would have to climb a ladder to hear them.

Ata, Attaboy this, The Turk that ...

There was the story of the burping machinegun and bank also known as the Robin Hood and the Pissed Boys story or the lots of new things for everyone story ... or the Speed Man story or the Attatatta-tatta-tatta-tatta-tatta one.

Theo's favourite story was the eighteen chicks in the one day legend.

You either believe it or you don't depending on your faith.

Theo's Mama didn't think there was anything wrong with a hero. She was married to Theo's Dad after all ...

*Ata And The Kids*

Wherever Ata hung, a lot of kids liked hanging too.

Ata was a real kid-magnet ... probably because he was so predictable.

Ata would stand still like a statue on his corner and make the noisy, local kids feel secure. All the kids would flock and hop around like sparrows. They'd run around and around and scream, their little kids' noses running and chant something like Bin-or-Bush-Bin-or-Bush-Bin-or-Bush.

Their hair was black and curly. They wore the same grubby clothes as their brothers and sisters wore before them when they played on the corner.

### The Food Chain

Theo was way down the food chain.

He just worked for Ata.

He was one of the little guys who worked in Ata's wholesale vegetable business or the Green'n'Gold caper as it was known down the pub. The business wasn't much of a secret unless you were a cop who hadn't earned some Ata money. Ata sold the heroin too, I believe. I'm not sure though. What I don't know hasn't hurt me for a long time.

Personally, I prefer a beer or a wine of either colour. Whatever poison gets the job done.

### Back, Back, Back

Attaboy turned his head as Theo tried sneaking by, carefully-carefully around his corner.

He just to check that Theo wasn't another hero. When he saw that it was just one of the daily riff-raff, Ata went straight back to cleaning his teeth carefully with a little finger-nail. He didn't want to chip a gold one. He bounce-bounce-bounced his runner on the wall behind him. He had things on his mind. He was off overseas in a couple of days with the other Turkish Boys in the Arfstrayan Brigade to fight on the side of god in the Gulf War.

Ata didn't mind a fight but he'd only ever skinned a knuckle or an elbow at most before. He might be copping a bullet in the head this time though. Ata wasn't the kind of guy to admit to feeling scared though, not without losing face ... His face was being torn off by a bullet soon though. Being able to read the future can be gruesome. Ata was unable to show that he was scared. He had to keep his local reputation. There was a price to being at the top.

*What's Wrong With The Truth*
What's wrong with the truth?

Nothing.

It's just not very useful. It can get you into trouble too ... It won't make you rich and if becoming as rich as possible is the point of it all, then the truth's useless even ... and becoming as rich as possible was certainly Oddy's major desire, especially when he was younger and wanted toys. Oddy was younger than himself for most of his long life and becoming as rich as possible was most migrants' dream.

*There Are Many Truths*
There are as many truths as there are types of people on the planet.

There's the little boys's truth, the little girl's, Mum's, Dad's, big and little brother's or the same sort of sister's, the ship captain's, the sailor's, the rich man's, the poor man's, the politician's which is barely a truth at all ...

You get the idea.

Truth is a good thing for speaking to power with ... Power actually fears truth.

I feel like a beer now or two or three or four or more. That's the truth.

*Sitting On The Toot*
I was sitting on the toot this morning reading my newspaper.

I get some of my best ideas on the toot upstairs in the pub. I could hear people talking downstairs in the public bar. The old people down there were saying things like things used to be better once upon a time. This old person's experience says that things might have been cheaper once upon a time but they weren't necessarily better …

I know. I was there.

## Tomorrow, Tomorrow And Tomorrow

Maybe tomorrow's will be better than today.

Who knows though?

Tomorrow hasn't even started yet.

## The Newspaper

The newspaper this morning was full of the same question.

Why?

You can only answer this question, whatever it is, with another question.

Why not?

## Rob The Rich

Rob the Rich was a very popular man down the pub.

He used to buy everyone lots of drinks all the time. Everybody liked him. Theo and I certainly did. Some graffiti slashed across a wall down the road from the pub said it all … *Rob the Rich*, it read.

## Breaking And Entering

I'm getting creakier.

Of course I know it.

The morning newspaper yesterday—I think it was yesterday morning—seemed to want to drive the message home recently, whenever it was … I know, I know. I can't even get my leg in through a window anymore.

*I'm* history almost …

Anyway, whenever it was the newspaper some morning

recently ran a headline in bold print that sort of insisted at me as I slumped on my toilet. *It's time to die*, it read at me. It told me that the likeliest time for man ... or god, I suppose ... to die was at the end of a week in winter.

I was reading this on a Friday morning at the end of the month in extremely late Autumn ... I got so upset that I entirely forgot I'm immortal. Wouldn't you get upset? Oddy was immortal too and *he* died.

Oddy *was* only half a god though. He only lived for as long as he wanted to and he was growing sick of being alive I think.

I suspect that he wanted to die so he just did.

Oddy was certainly growing sick of things like always being a migrant.

Migrants have never been treated like royalty in Arfstraya, not that Arfstrayans ever minded a queen as long as she was theirs and migrants mostly only get the company of other migrants, especially in Arfstraya. Add love of cards and small bitter coffees and Oddy's interest in the *kafeneion* is totally explained I think.

All the other migrants down there were probably only just as lonely as he was.

*I Had A Wife Once*

I had a wife once.

I lost her though.

That sounds clumsy, doesn't it?

You know what I mean though. She died. As a goddess she was known as Goddy Mama and I really loved her. She joined me in the mortal world where she grew old and died. She was called Moira there. Her mortal disguise was tough old blonde bird.

There's a Moira down the pub now. She *almost* reminds

me of the first Moira. The second Moira's a blonde too in a peroxided sort of way. She's always got her hair up in pink, blue and yellow rollers. She's my goddess now. Once-upon-a-time Moira enjoyed a mulled red wine made from grapes grown halfway up a mountain on the side facing the holy sun in a jeweled goblet. Public Bar Moira likes a splash of ginger ale in her scotch that she has without a straw.

Oddy was actually the person ... or god actually ... who invented the drinking straw earlier this century.

### Arfstraya Should Be Nicer

Arfstraya should be nicer to reffos.

People here have always been nervous about wogs. All migrants could use a friendly look but reffos really need a hand. They've got nowhere to go except a tent in a refugee camp *if* they're lucky.

Goddy Mama's million eyes are fixed on Afstraya and Arfstrayans. Cruel's one thing, mortals can do *cruel* easily, but stupid's something else again. Arfstraya can't be that surprised anymore by visitors even if they're just tourists who are only like migrants in that they're both not reffos. Arfstrayans should stop pissing off the all-seeing Goddy Mama. She's the patron goddess of whoever gets monstered. First Arborigines get monstered in Arfstraya, next it's migrants and now it's the helpless refugees. What's wrong with Arfstrayans?

It *is* my business. It's everybody's business ... Moira's not like every other goddess. She actually cares.

Where's my beer by the way?

### Oddy's Home

Remember Ata on his corner once upon a time?

The noise Ata made then when Theo rock'n'rolled around the corner strumming his air *gee*-tar wasn't a very polite one

... I can see it if I want to. It's brown. I can smell it too and it isn't very sweet.

## The Discrete Entrance

Theo came to the discrete entrance of a retirement home eventually around Ata's corner.

He slipped in quickly in case anybody was watching.

Nobody was watching what Theo was up to. Only Mama really cared.

He waddled into a foyer where the most beautiful woman Theo had ever seen, a real siren, was sitting behind the desk near the entrance.

He just couldn't take his eyes off her. A car-siren was blaring somewhere outside where someone was doing a Theo and breaking into a car. The noise broke the spell the woman's legs were casting on him.

She filed her fingernails intently as Top Ten hits played on a tinny transistor sitting beside her on her desk next to a lonely-looking typewriter.

She looked up at Theo with a smile. He just stood there ... forever if she allowed him to ... just staring winningly at her he supposed. She was just like every other chick he ever came across. She just ignored him ... Theo explained to her legs why he was there. Their owner raised a sculpted eyebrow at him and just pointed a fingernail painted violent red down a corridor yawning beside her.

'Odysseus is waiting in his room for you,' she sighed in her low, sexy voice.

Next thing Theo knew his next fortnight belonged to Odysseus. Drug-fucked Theo launched himself blindly into his future them.

## Disinfectant

The corridor smelt of a heavy disinfectant.

48

Theo's sneakers squeaked in the loud hospital silence as he sneaked nervously into the old man's room.

*Penny*

On his way down the corridor Theo passed by a nurse with her watch pinned to the front of her uniform.

She was stare-stare-stare-staring at him closely. Her head ratcheted around slowly as he passed.

'Can I help you?' she wanted loudly at him. Her stare caught up with him eventually. Theo was always getting attention from people in uniform. The nurse's name was Penelope. She mostly went by the name Penny.

'I'm on Work For The Dole,' blurted Theo at her.

'*Work* For The Dole? . . That doesn't make any sense.'

Theo stuck his hand out at her in introduction suddenly and quite startled her.

'Theo's the name,' he offered the silence. He got nothing back.

'The girly at the front said I should go straight to the old bloke's room,' he blurted on.

Penny stared even harder …

Time passed all-too slowly. He started getting double-silence.

'*Girly?*' she asked, glueing angry eyes on Theo.

'You must mean you'd like to go and see Odysseus?' she huffed.

He finally got the message. His back started to recede down the corridor. Theo's dumb persistence was quite a good quality to have at your back in a brawl.

Penny had been looking after the very olds all morning, cleaning up their poo, getting them their endless cups of tea and washing them gentle-gently with a flannel under the shower … There was just no patience left in her. She was annoyed. Nobody had bothered to tell her about this Theo person. He was just the cherry on top of a long melting ice-cream of a day now.

Penny groaned to herself. The boss wasn't ever coughing up for another proper nurse, she concluded exhaustedly in resignation.

'Do be careful with him!' she worried at Theo's wad-dling, receding back. Her hands just dropped to her sides.

'He's fragile!'

Theo just continued trucking on down the loping corri-dor. He wasn't unused to raising eyebrows. For all he knew he was heading straight into some fearsome giant's cave.

### The Place

Most residents in the place never met Oddy but seeing as they couldn't even recognise their own faces in their own mirrors necessarily they didn't really notice that they hadn't.

Even the barely conscious and very stoned Theo couldn't help noticing the smell outside the old man's room. It was a smell with a sound to it too.

'Pffffffffffffffft-fffft-fffffffffffft,' the old whatever went.

Theo let himself into Oddy's smelly room on careful sneakers. He must've made some sort of noise though be-cause Oddy looked up quickly at him. Theo worried that the withered old man's head would just snap off his emaciated old throat ... while Theo was still there.

### Pffffffft-fffffffffft-fffffffft-ffft

There was a whiff of disinfectant to the sound's bad smell.

The smell, which was more like one and a half smells, was mostly just stale fart though.

'Pffffffffffffffffffffffffffffffffffffffffft-fffft-fffft-fffft-fffft-ffffffft!' went the old whatever again.

Theo soon learnt that if there was a banana tint to the

50

smell it meant the breakfast part of the long day was over at least. A cold salami or hamburger with egg and bacon one with a hint of multivitamins meant that dinner had been served. A hint of banana-split junket and ice-cream with caramel topping meant that dessert had finished dinner. Lunch was anything still left in the kitchen that could go through a blender.

Theo learnt that you could smell your way through a day at the old folks' home.

The smell got worse. It reminded him of his farty, old dead Dad's living room after he'd got home from the pub where he'd enjoyed one too many glasses of rosé or beer after he assimilated ... So the aroma outside the old bloke's room was like some sort of trip into the past for Theo. The old blokes' claw of a hand was shoved down the front of his pyjama pants. In the corner stood Oddy's potty on wheels that Theo recognised from the time when his old man ended up on one.

'Pffffftt-ffffffffffffffft-ffffffffffffffft-ffffffffffffffttt!' ... said Oddy then.

### Around That Time

Around that time Penny would've been in a car home toot-toot-tooting like crazy in traffic.

She missed Oddy's monologue.

'Get getted!' started Oddy and exploded suddenly, startling poor Theo.

'You skid mark, you toff bastard!'

'It talks,' a dismayed Theo realised.

He didn't know exactly what to think so he just stopped thinking. This wasn't the first or last time he did that in his life.

### Oddy Was Young Once Too

'I don't have to touch it, do I?' the immature, young Theo

asked himself.

Oddy was young a long time ago too. He stayed young for a very long time just because he wanted to, I suspect. He could do anything. He *was* a god after all. He lived forever just about for instance. He grew old *eventually*. He'd probably had enough of being young.

Oddy sat up in bed in hospital when Theo blundered into his room and woke him from his long sleep. His flannelette pyjamas were buttoned up to the very, very top of his skinny old neck. Theo counted the few lonely hairs on the spotted top of him that looked like a speckled egg ... or a speckled something. Oddy faced the open window and felt the breeze. It was summer outside.

The very old man was making noise. It was talking. Theo listened hard.

'Pffffffft-ffffffffffft-fffffffffffffffffffft,' said Oddy. He looked straight at Theo as if he could actually see him.

'I-I-I-I-haven't-sat-me-down on a real white toilet thing for three-three-three hundred years,' the old man raved loudly and suddenly making Theo jump.

'I'm a toilet-toilet-toilet!' he continued. 'Dirty-dirty-dirty!'

Oddy began bouncing up and down in bed.

'Where's my junket? Where are my just desserts?' he wanted suddenly and loudly right out of the blue.

'Pffffffft-ffffffffffft-ffffffffffffffffffffft.'

It finally sank into Theo that Oddy couldn't see him properly ... or see at all. He was quite blind now.

'Pfffffft-ffffffft-ffffffft-fffft-ffffff-fffft!'

'Thank a god for that breeze,' thought Theo to himself. He could barely believe his eyes *or* his nose.

'You white-skinned, maggot of an officer cop!' cried out Oddy. The old bloke was swivelling his bald egg of a head now, this way and that. His skinny neck threatened to just snap! What Theo had smoked was helping him be jump-jump-jumpy. There was no explanation as regards Oddy except that maybe his battery was running down now or his fuses had blown. Theo worried that something might break and then he'd be blamed.

'Some-some-someone there?' the old coot asked suddenly.

'That you, P-P-P-Penny, possum? Give us a kiss!' the old Casanova continued. 'Pffffffft-ffffffft-fffffffffft-ffffffft-ffffffft-fffffffffffffffft!'

### He Hear

'Maybe the mad old bloke can't see but he sure can hear!' concluded Theo.

Oddy's hearing-trumpets were real whoppers. Each one was about twice the size of a mortal ear. The old man's goggles were quite useless. They were clouded with triple cataracts ...

'Pffffffffffft-ffffffffft-fffffffft-fffffffffffffft-ffffffffffft,' he said again.

### Old Tiresias

I remember old Tiresias well once upon a time.

He started life off as a man and ended it as a woman or not-man like all old blokes.

### Stammering

'I'm over here, Mr-Mr-Mr Odysseus,' stammered Theo.

'You're not *here*,' he had to explain to Theo. 'I am!'

### Chanting

'We-know, we-know, we-know,' chanted Oddy.

'Here, there, here, there, here, there ... same thing, only

different!'

Theo started to panic a bit.

'Come closer!' exploded the old bloke suddenly. 'I've never liked to do all the work.'

Theo slinked on over then nervously. He perched carefully on the edge of the old fart's bed. Old brown Oddy stretched his head in Theo's direction then, his grin more like a slash.

'Pfft-fffffft-fffft-fffft-ffffft-fffft-ffffffft!'

Theo had to wave and wave his hands. He thought he could hear laughter falling from the ceiling.

'Pfffffffft-fffffffft-ffffffffffft-fffffffft-ffffffft!' said Oddy.

### Once Upon A Time

Oddy's basic problem was just that he wasn't young anymore.

He was quite happy to see his last days out in a nursing home where he could at least get some of those sugar-coated pills he always liked so much. All the white-coated doctors who have always been able to rustle up one more billable procedure helped keep him alive forever.

### I Am A Camera

Some time in the past, last night I think, I started thinking pharyngoscopes talking ...

Greeks have always liked the idea of things talking. Greek mythology's full of talking things, animate or inanimate. Greeks just love the idea of talking, whether it's people doing it or things.

Imagine the pharyngoscope at itsy-bitsy, teeny-weeny, tiny-teeny Cyclops 3.2 pharyngoscope with its little camera beside Oddy's bed in his nursing home having a natter. Imagine what it would say.

'I'm shiny, I'm black and I'm very one eyed,' it might

begin.

'I deal only in black & white. I'm not sure I approve of even a shade of grey.'

'Odysseus, that hairy old pirate has no choice now but to swallow me, especially if I'm disguised in some white, fluffy bread.'

'Swallow! Swallow, swallow, swallow,' Oddy's nurses encouraged him. The doctors wanted a look inside him on the television screen attached to me so they might work out what was wrong with him. He'd started going to the toilet all over himself, to put it delicately. They thought that his insides must've gone all a-bubble. It was like Vesuvius kraking its toa down there frankly. His uvula was dancing around just like crazy and that was making him salivate all over his pyjamas. It's the alkaline pH in saliva preventing tooth decay, you know. Oddy's pH was obviously not doing its job too well ... At least tooth decay was a sign of life.

### More Down, Down, Down

'Was that still a digestive tube,' I wondered?

I could at least recognise his fore-gut sitting dorsal to the heart within the cephalic flexure. I could make out a hind-gut sitting in its caudal flexure which *was* getting a bit thin I thought. There was the buccopharyngeal membrane and a cloaca in its cloacal membrane.

'Jeezels,' I thought. 'Oddy looks like a big bag of shit from inside.'

He was clearly heading out on his last trip soon. I was just a thing with no sense of smell thankfully. That couldn't still be called a musculomembranous tube I thought?

### There Was No Point

There was just no point getting too attached to anybody in an old folks' home.

Oddy's nurses all gathered around the television monitor and sighed.

Even then the old pirate was stealing ... hearts this time. All the nurses, being women, were dancing to his tune, the beat of his heart.

'Tom, tom, tom, tom, tom, tom-*tom*, tom-*tom*, tom-*tom*, tom-*tom*, tom-*tom*,' it drummed. I millimetred past his pharynx, his oesophagus, his stomach, his duodenum, his jejunum and his ileum, his organs of deglutition in other words. This trip was an odyssey ... The end was just up ahead, where everything gets digested and starts making sense, where the small intestine empties into the large one. The caecum and colon come next, the rectum and the anal canal and inevitably and finally comes the holy of holies, the all-seeing eye, the anus, proof that Oddy was at least a bit human, the end of the trip.

## Omigod

'Omigod, omigod, stop, stop, stop!' I thought as loudly as I could.

Old Oddy was expelling me, he was spitting me out, the smelly old arsehole of a pirate. He was sat on the toilet by a stronger nurse. I wasn't too happy about getting my circuits wet.

## Do You Remember When?

It's time to change the subject, I think.

I remember being a child and dancing around Mama's bedroom in spiral spirals until I was seeing double and getting dizzy and falling back onto Mama's bouncy-bouncy-bouncing bed where I finally got to open my fat book of myths from Greece. Soon everything in my kingdom had a name. My white plastic desk and chair became the two clashing rocks, *Skylla* and *Charybdis*, my wine-dark rug became *Styx,* my chilly, lino floor became *Ocean* and so on.

### The Story Of Two Old Soaks

There were always these two old soaks down the pub once upon a time.

They were always down there. They just about lived there. They shivered together on their flimsy chairs at their unsteady little public bar table covered with quivering little puddles of beer. Everyone called them shaky and shaky sitting at shaky. They'd lean over at each other, take a big gulp of air and stay alive. They did everything at an inch at a time. Even one beer could be one too many.

Their stiff, old legs looked like chicken bones. I'd check my own legs out in the mirror in my room afterwards.

They made me want to eat more. I leaned over toward them so I might hear what they were saying to each other.

### Confidences

'You got to eat,' one old drunk would confide to the other.

He was leaning so far over he could hear that he was almost falling out of his chair ... His half a glass of shandy was rocked on the table.

'If you don't eat,' he was saying solemnly. 'You don't shit and if you don't shit, you die.'

These two old coots lived together just up the road somewhere.

Friendships between old fellers down the pub looked like marriage sometimes.

### Unbalanced

Unbalanced?

Me?

People down the pub think that I might be ...

I don't think so. I'm just a bit unsteady on my pins ...

Unbalanced looks like Cappy and his Bully Boys just turning up on the east coast of Arfstraya uninvited and unannounced waving their silly flag and expecting everyone living there to just drop what they'd been doing like having a life, get discovered and get conquered ... Of course Oddy was there as either a sprog still inside his Mummy's tummy or bigger and already a cabin boy on the *Endeavour* when Cappy Cook arrived in Arfstraya. That day went down in black history differently. They remember the day as murder.

## Spilling Blood

Personally, I haven't spilt any blood since that big Trojan War thing.

I'm not that bloodthirsty as gods sometimes are.

The thing I spill most nowadays is a beer.

## I Might Be A Pest

I might be a pest down the pub but I'm not an arrogant madman like Cappy was when he landed on the east coast of someone else's country just out of the deep blue sea and claimed the entire continent and everything in it, animal, mineral or vegetable for his Crown.

You may as well hold Oddy or Arfstraya's Arborigines themselves responsible for what happened to them next. They were there on the beach when *Endeavour* landed too.

Of course I was there ... somewhere in the background.

The locals rattled spears and shook fists at the invaders ... and some of The Boys pulled their triggers at them.

They were probably a bit spooked ... The Arborigines had already been there for ages. It's not that easy to stop The March of Progress. Cappy's Boys saw Arborigines as just savage man-eaters ...

Gross ignorance was ruling the day as it often does through history. Everything that day was just so historical.

### Uninterrupted Lives
The Arborigines had been living uninterrupted lives for ages.

Cappy and the Pale, White Ghost Boys just interrupted them though.

Sometimes a few eggs get broken or a few beers get spilt or something messy happens.

### Lower Order Boys And Higher Order Officers
Cappy was not the psychologically least complicated man.

He was a lower order kind of guy in a higher order kind of job.

He'd been sent down south to represent the Crown at the Transit of Venus and discovered Arfstraya while he was there.

### Using That Drink
By the way I could sure use that drink now.

### Anti
I'll tell you how Anti found herself on *HMS Endeavour* now.

First thing you need to know was that Anti had a gutful of life back on Ithaca as a perpetual inferior. She'd cooked her last hot meal there, so to speak.

She was strolling down by the harbour of Ithaca one grey morning, lost in depressed thought. She hadn't exactly been having a good time living under her brutish Dad, Ba-ba's roof.

She'd already tried to get away from Baba by marrying her first husband, a freedom-fighting pirate, Whatever-His-Name-Was but that marriage didn't last very long. He died.

She'd been stomping out of her thick Baba or Dad's house after a particularly bad argument at least once a day. She had to go and just risk he'd be smouldering with rage by her return. She just had to go though. A murder charge in those days wasn't just a prison sentence with parole. Her neck was growing unaccountably itchy.

She literally ran into an old sea-salt down the sea front on Ithaca harbour going by the name of Captain Bones who was also known as Captain Creaky. She went strolling down there for some fresh air and to cheer up a bit. She bumped into Bones and smiled at him with ... feeling. No one had smiled like that at Bones in ages. His thumping heart almost stopped. Maybe it did. Nobody would have known. Captain Creaky withered away in the end despite all the salt in his bones but before then he transported Anti to Plymouth, England with him. He sailed from there. Old Captain Creaky was a bit old as old coots went for Anti to have much fun with. He turned out to be the first good man in her life though ... except for her boy, Oddy. She had no time to waste. She wasn't an immortal or demi-immortal or semi-immortal like her boy was.

In Plymouth she found herself all alone when Bones shrugged his mortal coil. Anti never rested however often she found herself lying down in bed. She took up with Cappy in Plymouth and sailed with him on *Endeavour* to Arfstraya. Anti had decided that Cappy was a good man too. Creaky had spoilt her. Cappy wasn't a bad looker in his green'n'gold uniform either. He was still alive too, like she was in her less than perfect mortal way. Anti had already learned the hard way that a woman alone in those days was *very* alone indeed. All the rest is history now.

### Oddy Was Honest

The crew on *Endeavour* found little boy Oddy was confusingly honest at times.

They'd all grown up as street urchins on the streets of London before they were press-ganged into life on *Endeavour*. Cynicism was not unkown among them. Young Oddy was always giving things back to people who hadn't actually owned them in the first place. Not for the last time in Oddy's long life people around him decided he must be stupid or retarded or something. Honesty wasn't found on every corner back home where thieving was a way of life.

The biggest thieves of all at the time were the aristocrats. The full force of the state behind them wasn't enough for them it seems. They had private armies too. Oddy's near-stupid honesty was a glimpse into the ways of the rather slow hot and cold takeaway food man he'd grow to be one day who only liked lots of dollars if they were honestly made ... except maybe for the dollars he won at the races.

Cappy and Oddy were a bit uncomfortable around each other.

They *did* love the same woman.

### Sharing

Black Arfstrayans shared things.

The invaders brought the notion of private ownership with them. Nothing was ever going to be for nothing ever again. Everything was going to carry a price tag now. The Arboriginal way of life was soon going to be an ex-way of life. The Crown's pirates had brought greed with them. The visitors didn't want just some of the land, they wanted it all.

Cappy's Boyos had been hoping to find gold or jewels or something precious in the new land but these people didn't wear their valuables. They lived on it instead. They weren't just naked, they were *very* naked. The Boyos found them unforgivably primitive. No one deserved an entire continent all to themselves, especially if they were just black. The Boys had just spent many months upping and downing on the bounding main and were hoping for some booté as well as booty. They wanted a South Seas Island kind of adventure and what they got instead were inscrutable, primitive, degenerate barbarians ...

Even the flora and fauna on the new continent were strange which suited only Banksy the mad scientist. He was full-on aristocrat too. Gods and aristocrats do have a lot in common. He had his favourite thoroughbred smuggled on board in case he grew lonely surrounded only by social inferiors. Oddy liked any sort of horse at all as long as it was racing and winning dollars. Arfstraya was something of a treasure trove for him, full as it was of grass, roots and leaves which he liked more than people. Banksy went on to become an officer in the merchant navy where he could avoid ordinary sea riff-raff better. Oddy's Mum handed over all her hard-earned to Banksy to invest for her but the South Seas Bubble burst, the Sir Joseph Banks Bank collapsed and she lost the lot ... for the moment. Arrogant Cappy was an officer and gentleman of his time ... which meant he could be a real prig.

He became good at disguising his lowly origins. He *wasn't* an aristocrat.

Sea captains kept journals in those days ... Cappy wrote in his something up-itself like Arborigines were In Reality Happier Than Most Europeans, Being Wholly Unacquainted With The Superfluous. They Live In Tranquillity, he went on, Not Disturbed By An Inequality Of Condition. Cappy quite liked them, not that this stopped him killing them.

Back at naval college Writing Journals had been a popular subject though not as popular as Swimming was. These were sailing ship students after all. There was a lecture on trying to avoid being killed by locals in the Explorer Course, a fairly unavoidable occupational hazard. This was where Cappy learnt that he'd better learn how to become philosophical if he was going to become an explorer.

Naval College was where Cappy and Banksy became friends ... Cappy was the perfectionist or neurotic. Cappy was the more ambitious. Cappy won the prestigious Conquest Prize. This guaranteed official blindness in any new continent. It wasn't very hard to talk him into amending the official record of land-theft and massacre. Banksy was the one who always went out rather than study. Cappy almost *needed* to please his superiors. There must've been *some* backbone to him though. He *did* win Cooky's heart ...

*The Cook's Tour*
Go and get keelhauled or go and get flogged ...

Cappy had to get up in the morning from his warm, soft bed, untangle himself from his Anti's warm arms and pass sentence on his sheep-faced Boyos every morning after one last rock in her arms. Cappy had to maintain firm discipline. The lash was useful to the avoiding of mutinies. Cappy didn't have to like stripping the flesh off his boys' bones, he just had to do it.

A new day's sail could then climb up the mast. *Endeavour* could then take off and fly ... Who knows exactly where? The world was darker then. Navigation wasn't the exact science it is now. Knowing which direction he was heading in was the best Cappy could hope for. Guts were what exploring new lands in those old days of yore required.

All his Boys had demanded was a full stomach and no scrimping on provisions by officers lining their own pockets when they enlisted or were kidnapped and press-ganged. Ships captained by the traditional nobility were notorious for that sort of thing. Harbour front pubs were loud with all the stories.

*Old Sydney Town*
The crew of *Endeavour* eventually landed at Botany Bay and settled old Sydney Town ...

This was the very first time local Arborgines were evicted.

*Serial Monogamy*
Phil The Greek was Anti's next conquest.

She was such a serial monogamist.

*Revolution*
The blacks and the lumpy proletariat should've joined together and revolted.

The red-coats were such a common oppressor. I'm just not sure why they didn't. It would've made quite good sense ... but I think that the great Arfstrayan racism might've been rearing its ugly head for the very first time ... though definitely not the last time.

Bennelong should be mentioned.

He did prove forever that a tame, live, black was better than a dead one any old day.

*Tame Black*
Bennelong was Governor Phil The Greek's choice as collaborator.

Phil needed someone through which he could speak to other blacks and give them bad news after bad news.

It *was* their country. Phil The Greek had stolen ... *taken* ... it.

*Greek*
Phil wasn't really Greek.

He was just tall, dark and handsome.

Anti grew a bit tired of Cappy in the end, especially when he sailed back home to his wife. Anti had become a perpetual girlfriend. Phil had a wife back home.

Anti only used to be one.

## Dainties

Anti would sometimes leave trays of *filo*-pastry dainties on window-sills to cool.

She'd been slaving over a hot stove to bake *baklavathes*, *kateifia* and other goodies soaking in syrup for the officers' table. They'd disappear before they could even get close to any table at all. Anti was just mystified but she caught *black* plebs licking sticky fingers like a ship's cat licks its whiskers. She was upset, Phil was furious and he'd go apeshit and want to cover them in chains, throw them into a cage and hang them for good measure ... Anti stood in the way though.

She tried to explain to him that they were only dainties. He tried to explain back to her that the bad guys were only Arborigines. She just wouldn't listen though. Her little boy, Oddy didn't understand exactly what was what. He just knew his Mama was right and that was all that mattered to him.

## God In A Drink

God is everywhere ...

That's gods plural, though not all at once. A single god's even in a drink ... or vice versa.

There's every sort of story in a pub. A pub can be full of society's flotsam and jetsam. We're not all booze-hounds ...

I'm not absolutely typical. I speak only the truth.

## Everywhere

I was sitting in my favourite spot in the bar the other day

which is everywhere. I was lost somewhere in my own thoughts about the story of the young Oddy's epic stumble across the desert in the company of the local blacks. What happened was that Cappy and Anti were always getting lost in each other's arms. Phil loved Anti. Everyone did, serially. She had always been monogomous, again and again and again. To young Oddy, it felt like his Mum didn't like him anymore.

So little Oddy upped one day and ran away. Nothing mattered anymore. He was either throwing a tantrum or he was in a sort of mourning. Arfstrayan Arborigines were certainly mourning their old way of life. Cappy and his pale white ghosts had killed it forever.

They walked *about* into the white sun together. Oddy staggered on short, white, little boy legs. He never forgot the kindness the people showed him on their long stagger together or the warmth of the meditative, communal campfire and nodding off in security and warmth. He learnt all about time from his new people's stories and timelessness too therefore, about how the present stretches and stretches until it becomes the future or the past if you're looking backwards. Oddy learnt all about roasted kangaroo patties with riverbank fennel on a milled seed bun. He never forgot chewing the fat over warm stories with his new friends. He really liked being a son again.

On his long walk Oddy learned that human feelings were like train carriages, coming one after the other. There was always a next one. Sometimes life felt like a messy, tangled-up train-wreck but that was only one story or an anthology of them called a life. He also learnt much to his strange relief that everyone dies eventually although maybe he'd just been staring into the fire too long.

*The People Up North*

Around the fire Oddy heard stories about a people up north who worshipped Cappy, Ned Kelly and JFK. He thought that this sounded like a book he'd read as long as it wasn't just in English, not that he could read in any other language either ... I don't find worshipping any of that lot any stranger than worshipping a carpenter boy. There's no such thing as too many gods. Mortals *need* to worship and worship gods. In the absence of them, they'll worship each other. I used to have a wife I just worshipped ... in my mortal guise.

*Baby*

Oddy grew older too.

He got a first wife too which was more of a secret.

One day he heard down his *kafeneion* that his first wife, Baby, was coming home ... or whatever was left of her that is after the big fire or cremation or clean-up fire the big museum in town organised when it cleared out some old things. Oddy learnt this when the day's newspaper was read out aloud to everybody by some coffee and cards crony of theirs.

He'd already visited her in the museum where she featured in a big historical diorama. Arfstrayans were quite interested in Arborgines even then ... as long as they were dead. Baby had been stuffed just like the wombat in the next display, frozen with her friends and family grinding seed forever to make buns in a mock-campfire. Clichés were clichéd back then too. In reality when she was still alive, Baby had just hated grinding seed. Where Oddy lived was quite close to the museum and not far from where they met. Baby had been enjoying a tipple with mates under some awning in town. Oddy was on one of his long, rambling walks when he fell right into her arms ... literally. There was a banana peel or something else slippery and messy on the pavement. This sounds like divine providence to me. They started talking in a shy, clumsy, stop-start, word-less way. Oddy didn't speak English too good and Baby was often too drunk in those days to speak too good in any language. Oddy's looks were still dark and curly back then and Baby's smile lit up everything around her. I suppose they spoke together in the language of love.

Oddy didn't look like he was going to hit or curse her like white men usually did after rotgut or something alcoholic had been forced down her throat to get her in the mood, not that how she felt things really made any difference. Oddy was different though. He actually liked her ... He tried to move her into his latest boarding house up the backstairs. Oddy knew all too well what his latest *kyra* thought of black girls and he knew what country he was living in and in just what sort of esteem Arborigines were held. Even so the two of them ended up living together in *another* boarding house in another reduced, depressed and depressing part of town. They eventually separated but not before Oddy's extremely coffee-coloured first son was born.

Even a light tan was too much tan in the Arfstraya of those days. Oddy himself was seen as *too* tanned for pasty-white Anglo Arfstraya.

*Collecting*
Oddy wasn't sure if he could collect her from the wharves without bursting into tears.

He couldn't do much at all without bursting into tears though. That was the migrant, non-Anglo, ethnic, over-emotional wog in him.

Baby's real name and the real name of her tribe too haven't survived any more than her people have. We'll just have to call them Arboriginal, whatever else they would've called themselves.

### Oddy's Explorers

I've heard Oddy described as an explorer-groupie which isn't entirely wrong.

He wined and dined all Arfstrayan explorers, the great and the small, the long and the short. I mean the *tall* and the short. Arfstraya had more than its fair share of explorers of whatever length for just one country. Hungry explorers were Oddy's favourite sort.

Oddy enjoyed the lies or stories they told. He enjoyed food too, whether it was preparing it for someone else and feeding others or just eating it himself. He told a few lies back to them too, just to be polite. He'd tell them stories about life back home as just the little boy who brought down the entire Ottoman empire single-handed. He told his stories in Greek though. Language difficulties never stopped Oddy. Oddy's explorers got hand gestures and a fractured sort of English.

Oddy would've fed today's explorers too if he could've, the astronauts. They faced the great unknown. Exploring and astronaut-ing aren't that different to each other. They both take the same amount of courage in the face if the unknown. Being a migrant, being an explorer and being an astronaut are all similar and all involve new worlds.

### Ludwig

The first of Oddy's explorers was Ludwig.

People sometimes called Ludwig by his full name of Ludwig Leichhardt.

He was a migrant too *and* an explorer too. Oddy *really* liked him. He was sort of perfect. He was an Arfstrayan hero too even though most Arfstrayans wouldn't have described Ludwig as even Arfstrayan.

Ludwig was born in Berlin. That's Berlin, Germany, not the UK Berlin. Being born overseas isn't uncommon in Arfstraya.

## Hats

The official story doesn't talk about just how much Ludwig liked hats.

I'd say that Ludwig really liked the hatter actually. Ludwig was probably mad. He was always picking imaginary lint off his clothes, lint, lint, lint, lint, lint ... Sometimes he seemed like just one big tic. He liked order too, everything exactly on time, trains, orders for new outfits from the tailor, hansom cabs, everything ... He liked his clothes sponged, brushed and pressed.

Oddy knew him as L. Oddy and L became good friends. They didn't actually understand what the other one was saying half the time. They had exploring and storytelling or making things up in other words. They both ate food too. Arfstraya suited them both. Everything was predictable. The same brand of bread was often buttered in the same way with the same butter and butter-knife at the very same time *every* morning.

This suited L who *insisted* quite Teutonically and firmly on being a cliché. He clicked his heels crisply, he wore lots of very black leather, he liked smacking naughty, naughty bottoms ...

Oddy and L met in the park. Both their heads were held high firmly in the clouds. They bumped into each other and started talking in an urgent hand gesturing, broken English sort of way. A deep friendship grew between two lonely, odd birds. L was out clearing what he hypochondriacally thought was a consumptive head in the dry Arfstrayan air, so different to the dank European version. Oddy had his woven basket full of buttered cold-cut sandwiches for sale hung over a tanned arm. His product was quite popular. Oddy was soon on the way to his first fortune, the first of many selling food that he just threw away on the gee-gees. They recognised the perpetual stranger in a new land in each other immediately. They were both a bit *focaccia* in a white bread land.

## The Days Were Sunny

The days were always sunny in the clipped, perfumed and bordered part of town L lived in.

He'd always preferred to live in the most comfortable and exclusive part of town where the money all lived. Only rich people could afford takeaway food. Migrants have always serviced that relationship for as much money as possible. Oddy had found a boutique baker to make the Turkish *pide* bread buns and a nice tangy relish for the kebabs. Oddy had learnt early in his time in Arfstraya that rich, hungry people with high disposable incomes in Arfstraya would pay heaps for exotic things as long as they weren't *too* exotic. Oddy had invented market research.

Ludwig purchased a corned beef and pickle sandwich to takeaway from the swarthy, good-looking takeaway food man. He'd patted his tummy then to indicate that the food was yummy. L was wearing a delicately pin-striped, woollen suit at the time. Odd's look up and down through the dense mist of aftershave or perfume always hovering around Ludwig was a sort of congratulations over Ludwig's phat, phat threads. It was a bit hard not to stare at Ludwig who didn't look the way he did in order to not be stared at and noticed though.

Oddy lowered his eyes quickly to the coins Ludwig jinkled into his outstretched hand for the sandwich. Complimenting L on his clothes was no more a mistake than complimenting Oddy on his food was.

*Pants Man*

The gentle-ladies who'd see him all dude-d up and mysterious in the park and talked about him a lot to each other knew L as Pants Man.

Pants Man wanted to leave the city and go exploring. He really needed to lose himself. Oddy went to the outskirts of the city, shook his hand firmly and took the opportunity to press a keepsake onto him that might just remind him of his good friend forever. It was a used paper napkin from a takeaway roll that some punter had just scrunched up after a munch and just thrown away. Oddy hadn't invented recycling yet. Almost immediately Ludwig's eyes turned to the horizon ... The two friends waved sad hankies at each other. Oddy burst into tears.

*The Top End*

Arfstraya *is* a Big Country.

There's a Top End, a Bottom End and two Side Ends known otherwise as coasts. There's a red-hot Centre close to where L left for ... Even the air the morning Ludwig started off felt rare. Ludwig's step grew jauntier the further away from the city he got. Yes, he was sad to be farewelling his friend but he was glad to be going too. Oddy couldn't really understand why anyone would want to leave the city for a wide open, anti-city, country space. Oddy had learned a long while ago though that whatever was going to happen was just going to happen so he just respected his friend's need and promised to miss him.

Pants had come, saw, conquered a few lady-hearts and left to get well trekked.

Once the predictably temporary goodbyes and eternally grateful thank-yous had been said by him and Oddy, he was off quite happily. L had been starting to feel cramped in the head. He needed a good stretch and to clear his imaginary lungs. He'd been yearning for a less well-manicured, wide-open space.

## Moping

Oddy just went back to his lonely boarding house.

He moped around a bit and just picked his dustpan up from where he'd last put it down ... He left for his usual *kafeneion* in the city where he could enjoy his usual tiny, tasty cup of bitter coffee and play some cards. On the way there, he dragged his heels past the up-market private hotel where L had lived. He stopped outside and just lingered a while. He earned the attention of the local constabulary who were called by L's anxious, moneyed ex-neighbours. When he just sloped back home in dejection to his own more sparse boarding house when he finally got out of the cop-shop, he raised a cut-crystal goblet of something red to the memory of his recent past with his mate. Their landladies were both widows. One was Greek and the other one was Greek too but more pretentious. Guess whose?

## Back-slapping

Arfstrayans adored explorers.

White Arfstrayans loved thinking of their home as a mysterious, barely explored continent with a hot, empty Centre.

## Water

The local Arborigines could've saved L.

No white liked to admit that an Arborigine knew anything that a white man didn't. This was just in those days, not today surely amongst middle-class people. No one even liked to speak to an Arborigine unless it was another Arborigine. Arborigines and migrants in Arfstraya are similar only in respect of what they're *not* ...

They're both *not* Anglos.

### Go Perish

Arfstrayans loved a hero back then in those days too ... unless he or she was a migrant too.

My bet is that Ludwig will just be forgotten one day.

Oddy didn't even pretend he wanted to be a rugged explorer. He would have been quite happy to be taken seriously as Arfstraya's best takeaway food man.

### Losing Things

Ludwig will always be remembered for losing things gloriously.

He lost his place in Arfstrayan history as a *living* legend. He'd already lost his bearings and then he lost his life.

L was looking for a route across the top of Arfstraya. Arboriginal Arfstrayans already knew this but they were the wrong colour for being taken seriously as anything in the country. They didn't even make maps. They'd already forged all the paths they needed to a long time ago. They'd named all the mountains, all the rivers, and everything else up there, just not in English ...

### Carking It

L was very, very alone when he died.

He could explore Hades to his bursting heart's content. I've never been to The Centre. Most Arfstrayans haven't.

L would've given just about anything in the end apparently for just one glass of water. Ludwig thought he could make out his mate, Oddy on top of the next dune, a basket of juicy sausage sandwiches dripping with Dijon mustard slung on an imaginary arm. He was holding out a glass of cold, sweating Perrier or orange cordial or something long and wet.

Ludwig's end was altogether *too* sunny. His brain went liquid. Flies buzzed and buzzed around his head. L waved and waved his hand, his hand, his hand, his hand. He saluted and saluted. There weren't ever going to be so many flies in Ludwig's life ever again.

### The Real Oddy

Meanwhile the real Oddy was busy at home buttering and buttering the next day's juicy takeaway *kransky* sausage rolls and sandwiches at his kitchen table while Ludwig flailed in the desert heat.

L, known as The Kaiser around all the traps Odd took him, flailed, flailed, flailed and all too slowly came apart in the white-hot sun. He just stumbled on until the very end.

### There Are No Surprises

Ludwig's disappearance didn't surprise Oddy.

Oddy *was* a god. He'd already read the future. The desert had already been there in his friend's eyes for ages. Oddy had also read the dark smudges at the bottom of his friend's coffee-cup. The murky promises there were quite clear.

At their last supper where the food and drink was just excellent again, Oddy had gone very quiet at one stage.

Oddy forgot Ludwig eventually. He was a survivor after all. He was a migrant. He formally got the sad news over one of his daily *kafeneion's* tiny little cups of black, black coffee when the paper was read out aloud to him as usual. He couldn't read a word himself like most of the other Greeks there. The one who was reading the newspaper out aloud to everyone else was probably really one of those smart Armenians and could actually read. Oddy let out a sudden deep sigh. He already knew of course but there's always a need for melodrama at least for the audience's sake. Oddy put his best pokerface on and just played the cards he'd been dealt silently in the end. He did most of his loud sighing afterwards. He'd never be enjoying a sunny, parky day again with his friend or a yack over a glass of red at the bar in the pub or the even redder sauce the pub-meal would be soaked in. That sort of meal was known as a counter lunch later ... It was one of those few things Oddy *didn't* invent or discover.

### Yuck

There were explorers Oddy didn't like, as hard as it is to believe such a thing.

He just wasn't happy feeding such explorers even if they were starving.

Charles Sturt, called Yuck whenever his back was turned by the street scamps of the time was one of *them* ... Oddy was *not* an unfriendly man but he never warmed to Yuck. He'd always found Yuck to be the archest of all arch-hypocrites. Oddy just didn't like it when Yuck was about .

Like many white people at the time Charles or Chuck Sturt or Old Fruity as he was called behind his back again by the Mums and Dads of the annoying little scamps, could only imagine an inland sea in Arfstraya's hot centre that used to flood ... People back then just didn't seem to want to accept the idea of a ridiculously hot centre. It was like everyone had become a travel agent and just needed to hide the real truth from potential visitors.

Oddy was a god who knew everything though and he just knew that this was all a bit hare-brained and just not true.

### Wet Heart

I quite like the idea of Arfstraya's having a wet heart.

It sounds a bit like a medical condition.

Water symbolised emotion to the hippies of that time too … I can't stop myself being a bit tickled by the relationship between hearts and feelings. One of Penny's magazines was full of articles about the mysterious, dead centre and ads for those travel agents just mentioned.

*Old Fruity*

Old Fruity organised an expedition into the interior to find this watery heart.

A boat was filled with food, fresh water and lots of reading material. It also carried two of every *local* animal. He obviously thought of himself as a latter-day Noah figure.

Yuck needed to talk to a doctor, I'd say.

The animals would've been quite pleased when Yuck finally gave up.

I think what Oddy liked about Yuck was that he was a dreamy dream-dreamer like Oddy himself.

All Oddy disliked about Chuck was that he would've loved to be a hero … and reminded him that the hero and god times were over now and that it wasn't once upon a time anymore.

I don't really like the possibility much myself.

*Eureka!*

Oddy eventually took a swim outside his Mama in his shallow, tin bath.

He held his breath and ducked and ducked his head for ages and all that time his Mum was waiting for him next to his bath with a thick, warm towel in her arms just waiting for him. Oddy fell in love with a splish-splash again. The water swelled over the lip of the bath every time he ducked.

'Eureka!' he cried when he realised that his white enamel bath was just water quite un-ruined by salt and that he didn't have to be a little god to drink it and survive the taste!

Later when Oddy was taller he loved his Mama a-honking and a-tonking at the piano.

She had always loved playing the piano. She headed straight for the piano at The Eureka Stockade Tavern. She always loved getting people up on their feet and dancing. Anti had been a party-girl. When the piano started honking at Eureka, she swept him up in her arms and danced him around the room on the stamped earth floor.

### A-Honking And A-Tonking

I knew Terpsichore the party goddess well once upon a time.

Ask me no questions and I'll tell you no lies.

Let's just call her an old girlfriend. She always liked dancing. I can't ever forget Va-Va-Voom as I sometimes called Terpsichore ... She liked not wearing clothes while she was doing her dancing sometimes too.

### Outraged Nobs

The nobs of that time were outraged by the thought of drunken revolutionaries at Eureka.

The time had come to revolt and go Eureka. Crowds had started to gather in the streets. Oddy was out on the street one day with his proverbial full of his proverbial rolls and sandwiches slung on his proverbial arm flogging his proverbial wares when yet another cry of freedom went up. A small river of men started flowing. Oddy joined it with his basket full of wares ... A lot of people often meant good business. Business hadn't been wonderful. Politics had been getting in the way all day.

The word had been going around the *kafeneion* for a while now that the miners had been screaming ... in low, very masculine voices ... that enough was enough ...

It's hard to know what else enough would be ... You get the idea though. The time, time, time for liberty was nigh. Paying off bent coppers was expensive enough when you didn't earn much in the first place without having to pay an exorbitant amount for a licence just to dig a hole in the ground.

## It Was A New Morning

It was a new morning.

The night before six stars had blared out in an inky blue Arfstrayan night sky. This was a sign from my relatives, the *other* gods I suppose. Oddy had been up all night buttering buns, pacing up and down a lot and thinking about making food and money. Revolution was often caused by hunger then too. Lots of marching always made it worse. So in a way of seeing, buying Oddy's food was a sort of buying into the politics of the time. Oddy was happy to be feeding revolutionary masses too as long as he could make money doing it. There was something in the air that day as well as oxygen, carbon dioxide, nitrogen and the usual stuff. There were thoughts of liberty, fraternity and equality too. A small river of people shook their fists into the air ... as if the gods were responsible for all the inequality.

'Yummy, yummy ... pounds, shillings and pence,' thought Oddy to himself.

## Heady

Rebellion's got a heady scent that can draw crowds.

It at least drew Oddy though that might've been the seductive ratta-tatt-tatt of the rebel kettle-drum at the head of the ... mob ...

'Freedom, freedom, freedom!' it chanted the ... group ... of miners!

'Down with tyranny!'

The river of miners swept Oddy along with them. One of the miners caught his eye. Maybe it was the swagger of him, maybe it was the glare in his eyes or maybe it was the fact that his two eyes glared in two different directions. He wore the oddest head Oddy ever saw on a human being. Trudging by sternly was Al Niño, Oddy's great mate at Eureka and possibly one of the best friends Oddy ever had and a man of storms of extremely deep feeling.

## Al Niño

Al Niño was not a pretty man.

His complexion was like grated cheese, two wild eyes bulged like two olives, his cheeks were as thick as slabs of bacon and ham-pink and fatty white. Poor ugly Al was always having sticks and stones thrown at him by schoolkids who pointed at him and chanted Pizza-Face, Pizza-Face at him. It's hard to know what was more hurtful, all the stones he stopped or the words. He shared a tent with Oddy at Eureka and ended up liking him more and more the longer he did ...

## The Graces

Thinking about ugly Al insists that I talk about the most beautiful girls I ever met too.

The contrast is quite necessary.

The two Graces were identical, heavenly twins. I used to take a long stroll with them sometimes of a moonlit, magical night with a breeze blowing as soft as a touch. I had one of them on each arm. I can't ever forget the curvy Graces Girls. Nor will I ever forget one drunken night in particular ... No, mind your own business.

## Knowing Everything

Al always had to know everything.

He used to chant why, why, why, why, why a lot, obviously wanting to know why.

Al had some delusions that were much more exhausting than this one though. He was convinced for instance that he was Spanish and that the Spanish Civil War was on and permanent ... and it actually wasn't even going to begin for over a hundred years.

Oddy always made sure he always knew where the tent-rifle was.

The habit of Al's that probably caused most surprise was his explosive yelling out like some sort of shot in the air.

'Cojones!' he'd burst out with or 'Libertad!'

His strangest delusion was that he somehow controlled the weather. An upset Al Niño could be very stormy. The tent he shared with Al got very wet sometimes ... *on the inside.*

Before Eureka, Al had been living modestly on a slag-heap outside a town with his *mujer*, Pilar. He heard the cry of freedom and followed it. Pilar adored him but was quite pleased to see the back of him for a while. He could be very exhausting.

*Fat Wa*

Al wasn't the only good mate of Oddy's in the tent.

Fat Wa was there too. Fat would smoke heaps of lotus with Oddy, get the munchies big-time with him and get cooking a very special sort of Chinese food. You could eat and eat Fat's food and never be satisfied. Oddy and Fat often talked to each other in the language of food and never shut their mouths. The Anglo miners all hated Fat even more than Oddy who was at least white. The regard for oriental gentlemen at Eureka was not huge. This hatred in fact was not unusual in the Arfstrayan story. His yellow comrades at

Lam Bing Flat for instance were massacred.

Fat suffered from some interesting delusions too. I put his interesting hallucinations down to his lotus-eating and smoking. In one of his the most persistent ones, he thought ducks were peeking at him everywhere. This was his famous Peeking Duck delusion. Fat was a miner too and oppressed. The Stockade was for oppressed miners, not for oppressed *white* miners so Fat thought he should join the revolt and enter The Stockade.

Fat could really fight, unluckily for some white miners who tried to stop him. Fat was so fast, he could be invisible like the wind. He used flying kicks and finished his opponents off with moves like The Chinese Burn. Fat's best Chinese mate at Eureka was Hoo Fuk Wot who went on to become a star of the silver screen.

### Shuffling Oddy

Once Oddy was shuffling back to his home-tent after a long day's work in his takeaway food tent, *The Spitting Yeeros*, where exhausted, demanding miners could get an inexpensive, takeaway feed for dinner. They would always be wanting some more tomato sauce or some more mustard or they'd accuse Oddy of making one hamburger too spicy or another not spicy enough ...

The public can be difficult.

At the end of a day, Oddy would want to put his feet up. He was too tired for even a quick tankard at the pub-tent on the way home when a carrot-topped, drunken white slab bristled out and bellowed at him.

'Hey, wog!' he bellowed.

The oaf swung a ham of a fist at Oddy. This killer blow never connected though. Fat got there first. He caught the big Irish bruiser's fist and blinded the bully with a flick of his pigtail. He sent him flying with a kick and landed back on slippered feet, wearing the unruffled stare of a hero. He helped Oddy up then and earned himself a lifelong friend and all the greasy takeaway food he could ever take away.

## Lola

Lola Montez was the most striking woman Oddy ever met.

She was a great kisser too.

Lola liked being on top. What Lola wanted, Lola usually got.

One evening after a long day's work with Al and Fat in the takeaway food tent selling fish'n'chips and everything else, Oddy took a rare five minutes in the pub-tent where Lola was putting on a show. The piano was a-tonking and a-honking. You could barely hear yourself think. Lola spied Oddy from the stage, liked what she saw and snaked out her bull-whip. Next thing Oddy knew, he was being dragged out the swinging pub-doors into the rootin'-tootin', cigar-smoking, whip-cracking show-gal Lola's hotel room across the road. Oddy never did tell Theo precisely what happened next. He used the one word over and over again.

'Wow!' was all he'd say.

Lola Montez had quite a good singing voice the paper reckons.

## The Flag

That night when the sun went down, six white stars blared in a dark blue Arfstrayan sky.

This was called The Southern Cross and became the miners' flag. There was no union jack in the corner. This *was* a rebellion. Arfstrayan history was no longer just the builder's version. There was always going to be a builder's labourer's version now. The Eureka stars and sky were going to fly on the rolling shoulders of somebody striding down the middle of any Arfstrayan street like it belonged to him.

Back then on that first day the Eureka banner dragged Oddy behind it like Oddy was tied to it. The other end was tied to a big, hungry crowd ... ideally.

## The Morning's Newspaper

The next morning's newspaper barely mentioned Eureka.

Maybe its owner was some sort of media baron ... or just a baron who was only really interested in other rich people and their news. It just carried news about the Eureka flag's being up for sale again or whatever bits of it hadn't already been sold to some museum. The Eureka flag just flies on souvenirs now.

## The Foreigners

Oddy and Fat weren't the only foreigners at Eureka.

Al was from another planet.

There *were* British soldiers too ... There was Oddy's good friend, Raffy too.

Raffy was more properly known as Raffaelo Carboni who had been impressed by the fact that a lot of people in Arfstraya didn't have enough to eat.

A dollar's a very democratic thing. Anyone can own one. Some people just don't or have enough to eat.

Oddy used to like feeding Raffy who wrote bad poetry as well as eating up everything Oddy put on his plate.

Raffy wrote some quite bad poetry in English about Eureka. English was the lingua franca throughout the Stockade much like in Arfstraya today.

'There's no flag in all Europe half so beautiful,' wrote romantic Raffy.

## The Real Estate Thing

The question about Eureka in the daily dunny paper today

on the anniversary wasn't *why*.

It was *where*. The paper wasn't on about telling people interesting, useful stories *again*.

Where the Stockade once sat would be worth a fortune nowadays. Rates and tourism would both be worth heaps.

Maybe Eureka didn't change the future that much.

## Blood On The Wattle

Oddy got blood on the wattle.

Oddy hadn't been able to get to sleep the night before at Eureka.

He got up off his bunk and went out gathering wildflowers to arrange in a vase on a folding in the tent.

He'd hurriedly had to invent The Folding Table. He pricked his finger on a thorn on a wild rose. He hopped on one foot for a while and cried a lot.

Al blundered his drunken way back into their tent just then and a mad moment turned into a *very* mad moment then …

Oddy's hand was drip-drip-dripping blood over everything he touch-touch-touched.

Oddy was starting to grow a bit tired of living in a tent in Arfstraya.

Interestingly perhaps, one of the reasons Oddy *and* I both migrated at our different times was that neither of us wanted to end up living in a tent.

## Allegiance

The miners all queued up to swear allegiance to the Eureka flag …

Allegiance in Afstraya back then was more likely to be sworn to the British monarch.

Uniformed and well-armed lackeys lined up and got ready. The rebels checked their couple of rifles too. The latest Arfstrayan butchery was just about to begin.

It was all over very soon.

## Getting Away

The gun-play started playing and Oddy got away again.

Soldiers only shoot people riding side-saddle in a dress if they're enemy family.

The rebellion's leader, Peter Lalor had dropped in to Oddy's tent to offer him the job of looking after the rebel kitchen. When the rifle-work started, Oddy threw his rifle away. It went off when it hit the ground and ... The person that history could correctly hold responsible for shooting off Pete Lalor's arm was Oddy.

Apart from Pete, only a few miners on the rebels' side copped it. The rebellion failed. The establishment hadn't been that rattled. The British Empire had other colonies to call on if it needed them.

Al and Fat got Oddy quickly into a dress and onto Old Nelly. Fat chanted some Oriental words and spirited him away. He waved his hand and Oddy just disappeared.

## An Arch Big Conservative

Pete was quite used to never having to take responsibity for anything.

The establishment forgave him eventually and treated him like he was just a naughty little son of theirs. Back at Eureka, Pete had actually encouraged his lessers to revolt. He backed off then immediately and just went on and pursued a distinguished career as a political arch-conservative. Oddy went on to become a takeaway food czar.

## The Burke And Wills

It's hard to know whether Arfstrayans prefer a good mystery or a good story.

The Burky and Willso whatever was both. Their explorers always gave Arfstrayans good story *and* good myth. Not only did Burke and Wills explore, they also got lost, perished and disappeared … Of course Oddy was there. Burky and his Willso were also Bob Burke and Bill Wills, at least officially. Arfstrayans have always loved a nickname. The oppressively hot desert figured again in Oddy's life too. Oddy came across his old friend, the desert again.

I'll tell you the story.

## More Heroes

Burky and Willso were Arfstrayan heroes too.

They were also corrupt coppers. Oddy knew them both down the pub. He thought he knew them a bit *too* well. Everything that happened was *all* their doing. He really needed people to know that he was just a bit player. He used his mouth to let people know.

He hadn't invented the telephone and telephone directory yet.

## The Troopers

The drinkers down the local tavern knew them as The Troopers.

Oddy was known down there as The Wog. I told you. Arfstrayans just love a nickname and Oddy loved feeding coppers, even corrupt bully ones.

Oddy fed Burky and Willso a lot of takeaway so-called food outside the local. Oddy had diversified into *hot* takeaway and was consequently on the way to his next fortune, penny by penny, shilling by shilling, pound sterling by pound sterling.

## Lurching

The Burke lurched out of his regular tavern one night, an

equally drunken Willso in tow.

They discovered Oddy selling *hot* takeaway food outside.

'Where's your licence?' one or other of the two bullies demanded. Everyone understood the code. When they demanded Oddy's licence, they were also demanding a bribe and a free battered sav too from Oddy. Oddy had no choice. If he didn't cough up, he'd be spending a night in pokey. Oddy had never had a licence for anything in his very long life.

The Troopers and Oddy were old acquaintances. They'd been shaking him down ever since he first tried to sell takeaway food outside the tavern. He wore a hot-water oven around his neck now. A woven basket of *cold* sandwiches slung on a tanned arm was very old-time now. One night some drunken Boyos poured out of the pub at closing and came across the *hot* takeaway man outside. He was alone and he *was* just a silly old wog so they just bashed him up and took all his hot food. This old witch from across the road saw everything and rang the local cops. Bo-Bo and his Willso turned up. They were always together. They needed each other, not least to help each other find their way out the pub after a night out on the turps. They pretended to arrest The Boys just to keep the peace. The Boys were just being Boys and Oddy was a wog after all. It was clear that he was the one disturbing the peace just being who he was. The Fellers let The Boys go when the witch wasn't looking. They went *back* and bashed Oddy up again just to keep him on his toes. Oddy recognised The Troopers from earlier grafting days. They bashed him up again just to remind him how the world worked. They also felt like some more dim-sims and a hotdog each too.

### Land Of The Copper

Arfstraya wasn't Land of The Convict like popular gabbing would have it.

It was really Land of The Copper.

Why not? Coppers are as old in Arfstraya as Convicts are.

Paying off rozzers was an old Arfstrayan traditon. They could usually be kept quite sweet with the small donation of a tiny percentage of takeaway food sales or buying beers for The Troopers down the pub and giving them a small, regular amount of takeaway food. The Troopers wouldn't shout if the same shark as once bit Theo bit *them*. Oddy's shouting beers is another sort of investment.

### The Beginning Of It All

Governments, federal, state and local, in over-governed Arfstraya had offered a reward *to a white man*. Burky and Willso been enjoying the races a little too much.

They'd earned the attention of some angry local bookies with their own gang of roughs. They needed some money in a hurry ... so they girded their loins. They came across an ad in the front window of the local store for the offering a reward for explorers who forged a path across The Top End of hot, sweaty Arfstraya. Altruism and love of country were old-fashioned ideas. Exploring was done for money now. Camels and horses were fitted out and loaded up for a journey and finally got started in a dusty cloud of hoopla.

A crowd had gathered.

Oddy was there to see them off and he saw an opportunity to sell as much of everything and anything takeaway as possible ... as long as there wasn't any camel or horse in it.

### Wandering Aimlessly

The Troopers never got where they were heading.

They got lost instead ... bravely lost, but lost just the same.

They were such Arfstrayans. They hadn't bothered to talk to the Yantruwanta, the local Arborigines who presumably knew the country well and could've told them where there might be some water. The Arborigines were a kind and thoughtful people.

The dying Burke's head was cradled in a lap and he was fed ... even though he tried to drive them away by shooting at them.

### White Hot Sun

Every time Burky and Willso had looked up for too long all they saw was a blinding, white hot sun always ahead and an endless expanse of sand and ... a shimmering apparition of Oddy always just up ahead holding out a *souvlaki* roll and a glass of cool cordial. Flies buzzed around their heads. Their camels swam under them. The fellers bought a map of the Top End cheap from Oddy who kept wink, wink, winking at them mysteriously at the time. It was very rare and very exclusive apparently and *not* cheap. It looked just like an old piece of parchment that had been wrapped around a takeaway roll or something that some satisfied customer had wiped his gob on and thrown away.

### Frozen

There's a statue of The Burke and Wills outside The Official Museum.

Maybe it's a monument to stupidity. The fellers are perpetually frozen there in attitudes of derring and do. They're pointing to the future forever ... or to a tap or something.

### Parched

I'm parched.

Am I going to get that beer soon?

*Pissed*
Who knows?

Burky and Willso might've been pissed when they bought that map off Oddy. They did buy it outside a tavern ... Oddy had never said *no* to a quick earn but he never did see any of the money for the map from the fellers.

No wonder a copper's word wasn't worth very much ... *back then*. Oddy never did see any money.

The two fellers finally carked it at Cooper's Creek and became two more dead Arfstrayan heroes.

Everyone sighed when they heard the news. Even back then Arfstrayans were moved by a glorious defeat ...

*Ned the Kelly*
The Kelly family was another penniless, Irish family trying to scratch a living out of the dirt.

Like most ethnics in Arfstraya, they were oppressed.

Comfortable people nowadays with lots of money enjoy *the idea* of an outlaw and once upon a time you wouldn't have even bet even a farthing that Neddy would've been the one making the family name.

Oddy would've taken that bet. He was a betting man ... back then too. He would've won too. Neddy even become a national hero, even though he was once just a local hoon.

*Running Oddy*
It's not a well-known fact but Oddy once ran with the Kelly Boys.

There's a Kelly cult now.

It begs the question of why there was never an Oddy one though.

Oddy *was* a wog and Arfstraya was Irish-Land back then.

Ned still enjoys rifling the ghostly pockets of the respectable dead down Hades now. He's famous now that he's dead. You can even find his name on a brand of toilet paper now.

## Ma

Ma Kelly was the real hero of the family, I think.

There were a lot of Kelly kids for poor, exhausted, overworked Ma to look after. She was the one who kept the family together through heaps of thick and heaps of thin after old man Kelly walked out and just disappeared one day. Ma learnt to spread a shilling out about as far as a shilling would spread and still be called a shilling ...

Ma kept the girls at home while Neddy and the Danman grew up wild out'n'about instead.

Constant harassment by the bastard coppers was the last straw. The Wild Colonial Boys were just about to start riding ...

## The Kafeneion Times

Ma placed an ad in the *Kafeneion Times* for a chef who could ride too.

Oddy answered it.

Ma wanted to make sure that The Boys were eating properly and dressing warmly and everything else too. The successful applicant's duties would include getting the shopping done. Ma's varicose veins had been playing up. The job basically involved being Ma actually. She handled the interviews herself.

## Oddy's Clean-shaven Chin

*The Times* was read out aloud by everybody's best friend, a real *kafeneion* smoothy.

Oddy cupped his clean-shaven chin in a thoughtful hand over his slow coffee when the smoothy came to the ad. The takeaway food game wasn't doing that well at the time ... A game of cards would be happening soon but until then Oddy just twirled his fashionably waxed moustache and listened hard.

## Just Imagine

Just imagine what the Gang could've taught Arfstraya's Arborigines.

They could've taught them how to shoot a rifle for a start and revolt. That would've shaken up the British Establishment a bit. In return the blacks could've taught The Boys how to live off the land and freed them up a bit for more mayhem ... I think that the Kellys were popular because people's imagination was fired. There would've been a very different Arfstrayan history if one got guns and everyone had black expertise.

## Oddy And Kate

Oddy had to ride a horse though and he'd only ever bet on them before.

All he had to do though was just hang on and let the horse do what a horse does best.

Oddy and Kate grew keen on each other over time. A Greek was getting close to running with the Kellys. History doesn't talk about the fact that they were good, thoughtful employers either. The Arfstrayan media has always had trouble talking about labour relations or the fact that the poor make quite progressive employers. They know a thing or two about bad employers, I suppose. The Boys got a side-saddle for Oddy the first time the gang stopped somewhere with shops. They got Oddy tasselled chaps too and a riding crop for fun on days off.

## Once A Jolly Swagman

The most favourite Gang song was the one about a jolly swagman camped by a billabong.

He sensibly camped out of the rain under the shade of a coolibah tree. He sang while he waited for his billy to boil.

'Who'll come a-waltzing matilda with me?' sang the swagman.

This particular swagman just wasn't the full quid anymore. He didn't start off *mad*. He was *maddened* by Troopers.

A swagman's life *was* very lonely, just tramping up and down hot, dusty bye-ways all alone in a big country emptied of the black fellers who used to populate it, always on the sniff for even a trace of human kindness. The tramp's name was O'Kelly or McKelly. He was a poor Irishman or Scot who'd shivered through many an Irish or Scottish night with a wife and ten or eleven kids. His brood died in a mysterious fire. O'Kelly or McKelly had got on the wrong side of a local overlord, some Englishman given a land-grant by his Crown for doing its dirty work.

What happened was that he'd said *no* to the overlord when he wanted one of his daughters. His wife and all his girls all met sorry fates at the hands of the whatever overlord's Boys and the cops helped the rich guy. Cops have never cost much. O'Kelly or McKelly fled as far away as he could which was to faraway Arfstraya. He could just disappear there and drink the rest of his unfortunate life away. Corrupt, brutal cops are an all-too common theme in history.

## A Sip And Think

The tramp, whatever his name was and wherever he'd come from, would park himself by some water and just sip and think.

He liked gurgle water, I presume ... But just then a jumbuck came wandering down by the billabong ... up jumped Whatever-Kelly and grabbed him with glee. He was licking his chops ... and just then down came some Troopers too, one, two, three ... and four. These were Lonigan and his Boys, Fitzpatrick, Kennedy and Scanlan or something. They just about salivated just at the idea of a helpless old tramp they could push around to their bully hearts' content.

'Where's that jolly jumbuck?' sang one.

'If it's in the tucker-bag?' he continued, growling.

'You'll just have to come a-waltzing matilda with *me*!' he finished finally ... That was the fat sergeant copper who'd been angling for promotion and was already practicing being a real *almost*-officer of a bully. His coward-bully men rode up then too, also a-mounted on their thoroughbreds. They were singing with sheer dollops of glee.

'No, you're coming with me!' they each sang, one right after the other.

Up jumped the swagman then and sprang into the billabong. He had no other choice.

'You'll never take me alive!' sang he as he dived in ... and now his ghost can be heard if you're passing by that billabong.

'Woooooo-oooooo. Wooooooo-oooooo. Woooo-oooo,' it sings spookily. 'Woooo-oo, Yooooooo-ooooou'll come a-waaaaaaaaaaaaaltzing matilda with meeeeeeeeeeeeeeeee!'

### Dancing

Oddy wore a shiny suit, shiny shoes and shiny everything else when he went out dancing.

Oddy loved shining, especially if there were ladies around. Neddy was the Gang's fisticuffs champ. Oddy was the Gang's *lover* ...

One of them bowled blokes over a lot, the other one maidens.

Oddy was the lover one.

Danny was two bob each way ...

One thing he was definitely was the Gang's official mouth-artist, its official singer/songwriter.

Here's *The Wild Colonial Boy*, a little ditty of his and hit in its time.

Imagine music playing, imagine some punters drinking and carousing, imagine a roaring fire and finally imagine a pint of ale.

I wish a pint of ale just needed some imagining ...

*The Wild Colonial Boy*

Here are the lyrics of one of Danny's popular numbers:

There was a Wild Colonial Boy.

His name was Neddy Boy.

Dan The Man was his little bro.

Steve, Joe and Oddy rode with them too ...

Wild Colonial Boys.

*Chorus*: Oh, come and waltz matilda with me,

A-waltzing matilda, a-waltzing matilda, a waltzing matilda do.

Together we will plunder,

Together we will die!

Wild Colonial Boys

The Wild Wild Boys only ever robbed the rich.

They rode all over Arfstraya,

And withdrew money from banks wherever they went!

*Chorus*

*Hero*

As Danny discovered you can't go too far wrong in the entertainment business.

You can make a serious killing.

Arfstrayans love a hero!

Danny liked having a job. He went into politics after a career in bank-robbing. He was probably addicted to people paying attention.

## Odysseus Inspired

Oddy was loafing around outside a country pub during a break in his bank-robbing travels.

A drunk stumbled out the pub's swinging doors just then, tripped and fell down the wooden stairs and straight into Oddy's arms almost. Of course Oddy got a bit of a shock.

This bumbler turned out to be one of the most important people Oddy ever met. He was another god and he'd already spent his last few coins on some more booze. He certainly hadn't spent them on a bath or new clothes.

Oddy's nose had to work really, like the rest of Oddy would for a few extra dollars. Every single pinstripe of the drunk's vomit-stained suit smelled bad. He stumbled over the laces of floppy, unlaced boots like some sort of unfunny circus clown. Oddy spoke as slowly and carefully to the drunk as he was often spoken to as a Greek migrant in Arfstraya. He spoke in Greek though which was like gibberish to most other people.

Listening to Happy, Oddy honestly imagined that gibberish was a very appropriate language to be speaking in. He wanted to ask this gentleman who everyone around there knew as Hanrahan, Happy Hanrahan, if he could tell Oddy where a man or demi-man and demi-god could get something hot, simple, quick and takeaway to eat around there … Oddy didn't have the words though. He really wanted to tell Happy to just put in an order for something for himself to eat too. It was fairly obvious to Oddy that Hanrahan hadn't eaten lately. Everyone around there knew ole Happy. Happy Hanrahan was the local booze-hound. He slept everywhere or wherever at least he found a warm-enough spot. Happy liked to get around.

He was one of those rare white Arfstrayans who'd actually been outside a city. The horses were all loose in Happy's top paddock, so to speak ... History just doesn't say who mystified who more, Happy or Oddy.

They recognised the god in each other though quite well.

### We'll All Be Rooned

'We'll all be rooned,' Hanrahan told Oddy in accents most forlorn, rolling his eyes.

He was feeling depressed. Oddy tried to look him straight in the eyes. He couldn't though. Happy's eyes were quite crossed.

'Bedad, it's cruke, me lad,' Happy went on. He was hoping that the conversation might go back to something to eat, hamburgers or fish'n'chips or something.

Oddy finally understood that Hanrahan had probably been sent to teach him that he was relatively healthy by his relatives, the other gods and suggest a future for him. Oddy wished that he could make just a little bit more sense though.

'Begad!' started Happy.

### DIY

'Would you please show me where ... a man ... can get something to eat?' asked Oddy, always intending to get something for Happy too. Oddy was never an ungenerous ... whatever.

'Do it yourself!' exclaimed Happy, suddenly and unreasonably upset.

'Of course!' cried Oddy, suddenly inspired.

'DIY! . . Of course! How Arfstrayan!' he exclaimed to himself. 'He could do the food *himself* and sell it. People could take it away. There wouldn't even be anything to clean up then ... '

Oddy had just glimpsed the future! He knew it! Hanrahan wasn't just a booze-hound. He was an oracle, a messenger from the other gods himself!

Oddy reminded himself wisely then that people shouldn't just judge others just by their appearance. Oddy knew all about that ...

Greeks had always treated strangers well, in case they were gods ...

*Platypussy*

Back at the billabong things were going all platypussy.

The Troopers were yahooing, jumping around, yelling and shooting at the lonely, old tramp in the water ... Up rode The Gangsters then! ...

Neddy, Dan, Oddy ... and a couple of newcomer gangsters, Joe Byrne and Steve Hart. The mood thickened. If this was a film, the soundtrack would've just become louder. Joe-Joe Byrne and Little Stevie Hart were career bank robbers who joined up because they were addicted to adventure and money. Joey would pick a fight as quickly as some people pick their nose. Stevie Hart was more the fuss-budgety type. Everything had to be just so or he'd go berserko.

They were typical Arfstrayans as far as their diets went though. They ate lots of meat with two veg at most, if they had any vegetables at all. The Gang's diet at the time was a very exotic diet, thanks to Oddy, calamari in spicy sauce, fetta in filo pastry, roo au vin and rodent in a game fowl gravy, something richer than the bowls of watery gruel The Boys were used to. All The Gang had intended when it rode up to that billabong was to water the horses or a bush at most.

They found cowardly Troopers hassling a drunken old swagman who had just been getting a little jolly all by himself. Oddy was there too, hiding behind his horse. This might have just been the busiest billabong in all Arfstraya.

*Glenrowan*

Glenrowan was winning the Tidy Town award even back then.

It sat very solidly there in Arfstraya's deep south. There's a Neddy boom on there now. Neddy's become a tourist symbol. Glenrowan's got Neddy to thank for its entire economy just about, especially since the bottom's fallen out of more traditional rural activities like agriculture now …

Glenrowan's coining it again.

You can buy a tea-towel there featuring Neddy in his armour, six-guns blazing. There are things on sale there like a snow dome with artificial snow falling on a tiny replica of Ned and the Gang. You can get an imitation-pewter mug for the bar back home, barbeque aprons featuring Ned's good looks, postcards and all sorts of tourist trash with Neddy's name and his armour all over them.

Farming was Neddy's trade before injustice drove him off the land and he went all colonial boy. Glenrowan's where the coppers finally got him. He'd tried to make a five-fingered withdrawal at the bank there and armed Troopers waited for him with pistols drawn and rifles cocked to come out and step into the future. A-a-a-a-a-na cowardly flunky riding with the Gang, had tipped them off for the reward.

When Neddy swaggered into town, he hadn't intended

dying. He just hoped to plunder the place. Glenrowan plundered him instead.

## The Jerilderie Letter

The Jerilderie Letter should be mentioned at least.

The Gang stayed at the motel at Jerilderie I think for a rest.

Neddy got into a proper manifesto-writing mood there. He turned up the oil lamp, pulled out a quill, paper and ink and wrote the big J Letter. It became a PR consultant's dream. There was a pub there too where Neddy could practice robbing and a pub where he could relax, sink a few tankards, comb his beard, curse the corrupt police and their wicked queen to his black heart's content, river-dance like a fanatic as much as he wanted to and practice being a people's hero.

He had some armour made there at the armour-tailor's, a helmet, a breastplate, a pair of legs, a whole metal person in other words. He fantasised about striding down the street waving a flaming, cleansing sword, slaying the English dragon, ending poverty *and* tyranny and getting lots of things for his old Mum.

## Black Irish Moods

Ned could get into some black Irish moods sometimes.

He would've certainly got into one if he knew in advance how his name was going to be exploited one day and how it would become a sort of trademark.

Oddy got a premonition from his divine relatives and so he let himself out the back door before the big bang happened ... and no, absolutely not, Ma and Kate just weren't there at the bank. Oddy insisted on insisting. The Boys got shot up to bits or got frizzled in the fire afterwards. Danny was leaving anyway after just one last bank-job to concentrate on a career in songwriting and showbiz instead. They all followed well-armed and well-legged Ned into the street and the troopers let fly. The Boys got riddled and Ned himself came down in all that armour with a clunk, got arrested and put on show trial in front of a tame, talking beak and hung. A big crowd turned up at his trial and at his execution. The weeping Oddy never wasted a crowd. He set up a takeaway food stall and made some more killings.

### Time Again

The next episode in the Oddy story's the famous Heartbreaker episode.

Heartbreaker was a champion horse-breaker and an Arfstrayan hero too.

Oddy and The Heartbreaker ... or just Breaker to his very few friends ... met at a *barby over a beer* ... Breaker was more comfortably Arfstrayan than Oddy was.

### Setting Up The Barby

Oddy had set his barby up at the races.

He was selling *souvlaki* with yoghurt and cucumber sauce laced with garlic or *tzatziki* sandwiches straight from the portable *hibachi* oven he'd slung around his neck hand over fist. He'd make a few bob selling a few, whip the money over to the bastard bookmakers, lose it and then race back to his *hibachi* to sell some more sandwiches. The word had got around that there was no horse in Oddy's sausages ...

Breaker would have a sandwich, score a few wins, drink enough beers to fuel his confidence, lose a bit more, get some confidence up thanks to the beer and lash out on some *tabouleh* salad and *humus* sauce on his *souvlakia* sandwiches ... which was when Oddy noticed just what a rugged, handsome, tall feller Breaker was. They became firm *friends*. They shared an interest in the gee-gees, laying bets and then watching your money racing away. They ended up across a public bar from each other, shouting beers and telling each other pork pies.

Oddy put his foot down and said no though when Breaker asked him to wear a dress.

Breaker was better known then too as Breaker Morant now. He used turn a lot of lady heads and a few gentlemen ones too.

Describing Breaker as a manly man wasn't quite right in those days either. Describing him as *mad* and manly got things closer. Whatever people say he did, he probably did it. Breaker broke the news to Oddy soon that he was heeding the call of Empire to cane Boers and departing for Southern Africa. Oddy decided to take holidays and go with him too.

*The Killing*

The morning they departed, a rainbow arched over the wharves.

Oddy thought that this might be a sign from his relatives that he was going to be just fine if he went too. Oddy and Breaker were definitely not looking for the same thing out of the trip. Oddy just wanted to check out some gee-gee races over there and Breaker was looking for *action* ... a nice word for *killing*.

Heartbreaker may just have been a psycho. He joined up with the murderous, very irregular and barely uniformed Bushveldt Carbineers ... who eventually became known as the A.I.F. or Arfstrayan Infantry Force, just another British colonial force ...

South Africa was a tense place back then ... too. The blacks just watched as Brit white men slugged it out with Boer ones. Both of them were imperialist white men suffering superiority complexes. Arfstrayan still meant Brit and Breaker was a good British lackey who just wanted to fight against the Ottoman Empire, one of the other big empires at the time, just because he was told to. The only thing he really had against the Turks was that they weren't on his side. If he'd fought with them, he would probably have been known as Pasha Morant or The Pasher or something. Oddy had avoided all things Turkish since he was just a boy.

## Bunk

Greeks really have been everywhere, man.

Oddy woke up in a bunk on a ship on *water* heading for Southern Africa. Water *was* still Oddy's favourite thing, even more than tripping overseas ... *by boat on water.* The boat trip over to Southern Africa was like some sort of dream. The waiters were black and wore bright white uniforms. Oddy enjoyed the daily Boer-shape target shooting, especially after a few gins'n'tonic.

Eventually the ship docked in Capetown from where Oddy and Breaker trekked across to the Transvaal. On the way, dawn was a streak in the sky when Oddy heard a lion roar and a giraffe bleat.

## Bush

Breaker went bush almost as soon as they docked.

Oddy put on his apron, stayed behind in the flat and took care of the cooking, the sweeping, the washing and the sewing. Dinner was always ready on the table in case Breaker ever turned up unexpectedly. Oddy grew bored always having to eat alone.

He didn't have to do all the most menial jobs though like wogs had to do back home. The blacks were the underclass in South Africa. As Oddy soon discovered, there was no *kafeneion* full of Greeks in the city where a man could enjoy a coffee and play some cards. Oddy stayed home, grew a bit depressed and grew zits.

## Left

Left to his own bloodthirsty devices, Heartbreaker just got into trouble for butchering prisoners this time ...

His victims *were* only Boers and everyone butchered prisoners. At worst, his behaviour earned him a stern, monocled eye before and there was nothing in writing which was how official authorities usually stayed official. Denying all responsibility had always been very useful.

## Harry Was Unlucky

Harry was a bit unlucky.

He was only a sort-of-Brit.

People who could appreciate clean-cut, chisel-featured heroes like him would soon be holding his kind up enough as examples of a better future ...

He was a man born out of his time-time-time.

I shouldn't exaggerate though.

Nothing really changed *that* much. War was still war and it was still ugly. Someone smaller than someone else was still getting pushed around. Breaker was an unofficial sort of psycho. He wasn't an official psycho like Lord Kitchener, the Queen's officer officially leading the Carbineers in the fight against the Boer. Kitchener was just about groaning under the weight of all his medals and was something of an aristocrat amongst psychos. He'll be turning up again soon in the story of Oddy. Maybe he was another god.

Whatever though, he wasn't averse to a bit of prisoner-butchery himself. He was an officer and a gentleman though so whatever he did he did courageously.

*This Was Not A Pretty Time*

This was just not a time full of pretty mortals.

Massacre was the order of the day.

I was there.

At least Harry was court-martialed before he was dispatched. The appearance of things was important in those days too. This was a time when it was best to do even barbarous things exactly by the book. Breaker went out like an Arfstrayan, stiff-backed and square-shouldered according to the official myth. He spat in the face of the officer toff who wanted to tie his blindfold on so he wouln't have to look at the coming firing squad which was just taking orders too.

A second inferior tradition says that Harry wailed like a slump-shouldered bitch in the end.

Whatever the truth, a lonely Oddy was back home counting dinners again soon.

A vision in his soup told him all he needed to know about Breaker in the future. Breaker would always be in the past now. Oddy just had to forget him and get on with ... being alive.

The fact was that Oddy was always prone to being philosophical and just accepting whatever. He brought home all he really wanted from Southern Africa in his leather suitcase, some oleander and protea cuttings for his garden. One day back down the *kafeneion* again *at last* the newspaper was read out aloud to everybody just like it always had been and Oddy found out that his mate would be lying in an anonymous, foreign field forever.

Oddy just took a long, deep breath, sipped coffee and just got on with just getting on.

*Steam*

The steam was building in Odd for a while. The steam

was building up in the kafeneion's coffee-urn too. Oddy just had to get out of the house one day. The steam was built up in the *kafeneion*'s coffee-urn too.

One morning at last, after months of boring, black depression, Oddy chugged out of his latest boarding house whistling.

He started living for the day again like the young man he still was.

### Crazy Daisy

The desert in the Centre featured in Oddy's life a lot.

It was just like another friend of his. Daisy Bates, an Arfstrayan hero or heroine rather, Oddy's first wife lived there for a long time. Oddy had always found Crazy Daisy Bates as she was also known really hot. Oddy had first met Daisy formally at Breaker's funeral-do back home after his sad but unsurprising departure. She was married to Breaker when Oddy and she first met. They sort of twinkled at each other but Oddy was always a stickler for proper behaviour especially in matters of the heart or lap. When Breaker died Crazy finally made room for Oddy to move in with her ... He did.

Oddy looked Daisy up when he got back from Southern Whoop-Whoop. He picked up Daisy's sizeable bar-tab at the funeral do as a sort of nod to his old mate. The session with Daisy down the pub that followed was all it took. Oddy would be picking up Daisy's tab for the forseeable future and Daisy *did* like a drink.

### Crazy D-D-D-Daisy

Things started as just a drunken, little flingy thing fuelled by the old kickapoo juice.

Oddy fell in love and took Crazy and her drinking under his wing.

She was a very energetic dancer after a couple of beers. This was how she seized Oddy's attention. She pushed her bustle into his face down the pub at the Breaker do. She always thought he was a great kisser.

## Kabbarli

Daisy was called *Kabbarli* or Grandmother by the Arboriginal people of The Centre.

They succeeded in keeping her off the grog and giving her a reason to be alive.

Crazy Daisy did have an unfortunate habit of talking about *her* Arborigines like they were her children. She also talked about them as a *vanishing race* and she did seem to be able to live with the genocidal policies of the day's governments but that was because she really did want to *smooth* their *dying* pillow as she put it.

Governments of the day were pleased there was a Daisy. Arboriginal mothers did hide their children from Daisy in case she noticed the light-skinned ones. Daisy *was* unable to appreciate the larger story, why those kids had a light skin. Maybe she found the rape and abduction with impunity allowed at the time too unpleasant as a subject to think about but I really don't find accusations of collaboration levelled nowadays by cynical types who think that today's standards can just be applied to once upon a time with any sort of fairness just wrong ... I do think they're missing the most important point though ... I just forget what it was at the moment.

## Saviour

Black people at the time certainly needed some sort of saviour.

I honestly think that the worst thing Daisy can be accused of was being an arch white, Anglo woman of her time.

She actually came from Anglo-Land itself. She was a migrant, just like Oddy. Oddy told Theo that he wished she was still alive. He never forgot her.

## Big Daddy

Arfstraya had been alive for only a hundred years.

People saw that as a huge achievement or something back then once upon a time. Oddy went to the big public birthday party. It was called *Federation*. He thought it was called *Fetta Nation* or something.

He slung his usual basket of goodies, hot ones now, over his arm and went along.

A lot of people were selling things there and making money happily. Selling things and making money have always been very Arfstrayan pursuits. Oddy was certainly always happy doing that. He was still a reasonably young man in those days even if he'd already been alive for longer than most mortals are. He'd already enjoyed a good innings as they say. He'd already been at the crease for a long time, just to continue the silly cricket analogy.

## Cricket

I've always enjoyed watching the cricket on my teev over a beer upstairs in my room.

That's pretty Arfstrayan of me, isn't it?

## On The Moon

Oddy had recently been on top of the moon ... not literally of course.

He'd just fathered *another* son with his one and a half this time, his *second* wife, Beryl Markham, possibly the greatest love in Oddy's long life ... so far. All Oddy's loves were the greatest love of his life so far.

Beryl was definitely *the* greatest aviatrix of *all* time, even greater than that Amelia Erhardt woman which just showed what good PR could do, especially if you were an American. Beryl was only an Arfstrayan.

After a couple of drinks once Oddy described Beryl's kisses to Theo as like red, red roses, whatever that means. He obviously adored her and she adored him too. When she did fly off into the sky eventually and just stayed up there, they'd already spent what was a lifetime for most other people together. Oddy couldn't ever help but look up into the sky everytime he heard a plane whining up there. His Beryl-Beryl was the one in his dreams whenever horses weren't racing there instead.

Unkind people described Beryl as flying the coop and leaving him, Oddy once admitted despondently to Theo after a few more.

### Oddy Confused

Oddy grew confused at one stage.

Beryl-Beryl was growing older and whiter than him.

He'd just forgotten who he really was for a moment.

Theo listened, nodded and just nodded off apparently. I reckon he'd been smoking some of that whacky tobacco.

### Henry Parkes

Beryl was never as good a cook as Oddy was he once admitted to Theo …

No one was.

Oddy and Beryl called their son Henry Parkes after her Dad, Henry Parkes the butcher. The boy was mostly called by his nickname, Hazza.

Oddy heard Beryl saying that her Dad was called Hairy which startled him a lot because that was an old family name of Oddy's too. When Henry turned twelve he grew the full beard he became known by later.

Stroking and stroking one's beard was a common activity for some people in the days before TV, if you were a man. Some years later when Hazza fell into bed after his usual lots of late brandies and never got up again, Oddy was heartbroken.

Oddy was very fond of his boy. He was proud to be the Father of the Father of Federation ... so Oddy was the *Grandfather* of Federation, its Very Big Daddy.

### Word-hole

Hazza first made his Fetta Nation speeches when he was still young.

Hazza had always loved using his word-hole.

Oddy had always loved listening too luckily. He was proud of his boy's nation-building rhetoric even if he didn't really understand any of it. Hazza declared, declared and declared when he was a kid. He declared that the nation he'd build one day would last forever and would be a lighthouse of liberty, *the* beacon in the south. He clutched his belt, flicked hair out of his eyes and flung his arm out and out in salute. Oddy just smiled and nodded dumbly and nodded off eventually ... It was just as well that Hazza never actually required his audience to be awake.

### Fancy Ideas

Beryl had some fancy ideas thought Oddy.

She only wanted polished oak furniture. She also wanted an uppity private-school education for Hazza. Oddy was afraid that Hazza would develop some stratospherically high airs but Beryl just didn't want a common anything.

Poor Oddy worried that just selling hamburgers and kebabs for a living to keep Beryl and Hazza in the style to which they were becoming accustomed was maybe just not salubrious enough ...

Beryl would sigh and hang her apron up in the kitchen together with her dreams. Rifts were starting to rift between her and Oddy. Hazza probably got his blindest ambition from his Mum. From his Dad he got a toy plastic gun one birthday once. Plastic was a rare thing worth a lot of money.

Oddy had only just invented plastic.

### Fetta Nation

The crowd at the big Federation gig was huge.

Oddy got very excited at the idea of selling heaps of takeaway. He'd been up most of the night before buttering buns, making salads and getting his house in order, so to speak. The *kafeneion* had been buzzing with news of the big Fetta Nation gig for ages. On that day being a New Arfstrayan was just a good thing. The ladies promenaded in their best buttons and bows in a new day's sun. They turned parasols in the green and flowery everything in front of the new Parliament House. Their toff husbands promenaded in their toff hats ... their top hats, I mean. Every member of the lower orders was out and about too, scruffs japing japes, just everybody ... It was a day out for the whole, big, glorious mess of everybody, everybody a new Arfstrayan now. Everybody's dreams mixed with everyone else's and baked in the same sun. Dreams are dreams and is just dirt dribbling through one's fingers.

### The Weighty Hand

A big government trooper's weighty hand clapped hard onto Oddy's shoulder.

His good day ended then and his bad day began.

### Twit

Oddy hadn't bought a licence to sell food *again*.

He was trying to save some money.

'Twit!' he told himself but it was already too late.

## Licences

Arfstrayans loved a licence.

You need a licence for just about everything.

'Twit!' Oddy cursed himself again ... That *is* only a rough translation for what he actually called himself. Oddy could run like one of his horses if he had to ...

The copper marched him downs the Big House's royal green and gold corridor. A liveried tipstaff waved the trooper over and Oddy went with him. The tipstaff looked worried. Some lord's son or lord-ette out from the Mum country visiting the colony had just collapsed and was foaming at the mouth, unused as he was at the indelicate strength of the new country's sun. The trooper propped Oddy and his tray of goodies up against the wall and ordered him to wait there in a stern British voice. Oddy actually waited for a while. A British accent could be quite commanding. Along came another lord and pointed to one of Oddy's sandwiches and jingled coins into Oddy's suddenly outstretched hand and next thing Oddy knew he was in the big chamber itself with his tray surrounded by hungry lords. He moved heaps of felafel and taramasalata sandwiches in a small number of minutes.

## Just A Penal Colony

Arfstraya was still close to being just a penal colony of the Mother country.

It was already a nation!

Oddy was growing older too. Beryl made him feel young but he could never be young enough. She'd wake slowly in the morning, smile-smile at him and open her warm arms and white legs to him.

Oddy got into the House of Dreams that first Arfstraya Day where a mess of hungry parliamentarians had been up on their feet all day thanks to a copper. He made a killing ... He clapped eyes on his Hairy too.

### Unexpected Twists And Crazy Turns
Life's full of unexpected twists and crazy turns sometimes.

Oddy had been just expecting a thumping from a peeved trooper behind a wall and he got home to Beryl with a story about their boy who had grown up now and left home so that the house was feeling a bit empty now.

### Hazza And The Birthday Do
There's an oil-painting of the new parliament opening by that Tom Roberts.

The painting depicts toffs noblesse oblige-ing each other in their new parliament, puffing on their cigars and glooming up the joint, hobnob-bing and doffing toff hats. Cigar-smoking was a popular activity back then.

That's the starving in a garret artist, Tom Roberts, not the butcher one. Oddy knew him as Tommy. They met in a park and Oddy took him home for a feed. Tommy or Tom-Tom used to describe Oddy as an inspiration when he finally cracked it big. Oddy used to give him cups of tea and jam sandwiches. Tommy's in Hades now giving shades the shade-shits. Who better to look after an artist's interests than the artist himself ... or herself of course?

### Tom Roberts
Tommy's better known as Tom Roberts now.

Rich people pay the heaps for his paintings now. This was due to Oddy.

The other gods sent that single ray of sunshine slicing through the gloom as a hello to Odd. The painting Tom did is one of those works that tells you just who you are. You either see the gloom or you see the sunlight.

## The Inside

It just wasn't possible to know whether it was sunny outside from inside The Big House.

The Lords had been stuck inside doing their duty to their new nation all day and giving thanks that their new nation was making them even richer. Tom-Tom liked to pretend to himself that he was one of his betters too. He knew which side his bread was buttered and jammed on. He was no slouch about currying favour with the rich and powerful. He painted them, their wives, their children, their houses, their lawns, their parliament, their cats and doggies too, all their chattels in fact. He became quite rich himself. Oddy could've used a hand from Tom a couple of times because of his bookmaker troubles but Tom-Tom was always too busy to talk to him. He had new friends now …

## Plonk

The first Arfstraya Day was a day of plonk as well as a day of sunshine.

The lower orders covered the green grass with piles of vomit on that picnic of a day. The nobs inside drank fine wines from cut-crystal goblets rather than the pewter mugs lesser citizens used. They sipped and threw up delicately in some poor aspidistra in a corner.

## Look

Look over there by the side.

Who do you reckon that little guy shouldering the tray of full of sandwiches, stepping around steaming piles of aristocrat chuck is? Of course Oddy was there. People of all orders in the new country and new century get hungry, especially if they spend heaps of energy swanning around craning their necks to check each other out. This could've been the most energetic thing that many of them had done in a while.

### Squeak

While Oddy was selling *souvlaki* sandwiches hand over fist, he kept his eyes peeled for cops.

He was also hoping to glimpse Hazza. He could *hear* him. Hazza was thundering the *One Nation Under God* speech he'd heard a million times before. The boy obviously took after his Mama Oddy decided. She was good at propaganda too. He strained and strained to catch his boy's eye. He realised then that Hazza was actually trying to avoid his sandwich-selling Dad. A revelation that the father of One Nation's founder was a wog would be very bad publicity indeed. Oddy, usually a placid man just lost it then! One demand after the other in his ear in demanding toffee accents frazzled him when all he wanted to do was make a fortune. He snapped and sent his empty tray flying straight at Hazza. It missed thankfully and decked the premier of Her Majesty Queen Victoria's Colony of Victoria who was standing next to him. A pack of coppers rushed him like drooling bloodhounds. He knew what was coming next from the uniforms' polished sticks and unpolished boots. Oddy piss-bolted down the green'n'gold corridor and straight out heavy double-doors into the crowd rocking and roiling outside. He hurry, hurried straight home then into Beryl-Beryl's arms. Their boy mattered more than a new country could.

### Hezza

There was a Hezza in Oddy's life as well as a Hazza ...

There was a passable story-writing one as well as the Arfstraya-founding one. Hezza the story-writer was happy-enough with just a sense of smell, so he could stop treading

116

repeatedly into the pile of smelly doggy-poo in the barking alley outside his front door. Hezza was known as Lawsy in the innumerable pubs he frequented. He lived in rather reduced circumstances in a rather reduced part of town he was broke so much. For Hezza having nothing meant having *absolutely* nothing. Hezza is probably better known now as Henry Lawson, a kind, gentle drunk. The cruel world out there could be a *very* cruel world. It was good that he couldn't see horrible things in the world. The old days were not always golden. Yesterday was at least cheaper. Living people can be very expensive.

## Three Sheets To The Wind

Hezza could probably have written better fiction if he wasn't always three-sheets-to-the- wind. If there was a beer around, then Hezza insisted it had to be drunk.

People back then loved his stories. They would be called something like *lifestyle* copy now. Hezza's stories were set in a romantic outback full of romantic Arfstrayans called *the bush*, of most interest to yuppy city-dwellers driving their four-wheel-drive wagons or drays.

## Conservative

Hezza's stories were full of explorers, pioneers, patriots, un-tamed land, *white* pioneers and England.

It wasn't a magazine his stories were published in. It was a comic.

Some crony down the pub would read the magazine out loud to him. His interest in the bush was a bit hard to understand. Hezza was just too blind to go into the bush himself. Apart from anything else, he found even cows frightening. Hezza's stories full of the bush in that magazine which seemed quite interested in making it all up were very popular. People say that history's written by the winners. Hezza proved that losers wrote it too.

*See*

Hezza's blindness was a gift from the gods.

He just didn't have to look at anything he didn't want to see ... It was bad enough that humans did some things, without having to look at them being done too.

The gods love a joke, good or bad ...

Hezza wasn't just a harmless old drunk though. He could turn all that chattering and laughter from upstairs into stories.

It was lucky that Hezza was mostly happy enough with a bottle for a friend. A bottle never lets you down. People would usually tut-tut and turn away from the lonely, old drunk talking to himself while he was alive and might've enjoyed the company. He was just a blind-drunk, a deaf-drunk, smelly, dreamy, old alky write-off frightening the kids and often had his hand out annoyingly for any stray pennies

Ironically, Hezza's stories are usually about people. Lucky people who like reading about their own kind doing things they've never done and living in places and at times they wouldn't ever live in.

Hezza was very good at the look of places, at *exterior* decoration as well as well as the once-upon a time inside of a hovel back then or *interior* decoration. City slickers liked the subject of décor of the *interior* or *exterior* sorts in those days too. People back then didn't like blowies or brown snakes and that sort of thing back then than people nowadays do ... Life away from the city has always had its attractions though ... I suppose.

Luckily, people have always felt that whatever they haven't got or do is somehow more *authentic*. Hezza was one of the people from back then who got the benefit of people's need for ... *authenticity.*

## Romance

Romance has always been a popular genre.

You can almost feel the heat in Hezza's stories. You can just about smell the manure. He really was a very good writer. What you can mostly smell in them them though was cigar-smoke. It came from the cigars the magazine's editor liked. He used to puff on one while he'd lounge back in the plush leather chair in his office on the fifth floor of a tall building on the eastern edge of the city as he perused articles about Empire and a Very White Arfstraya emptied of chinks, boongs and wogs. Hezzy's fiction about rugged Arfstrayan bushmen and their stoical wives living in the isolation of the bush seemed to fit this magazine's mix well.

## *Isolation*

Hezza knew all about loneliness and isolation ...

So did Oddy.

This was just one of the things they shared.

Hezza's stories were often covered in ink-blots. His pages were just about painted. So when the newsagent felt sorry for him and pulled an ad out of his front window calling for a house-painter's off-sider Hezza got very excited. There was no welfare state back then in those days; his canvas would be as big as the entire side of a house ... Oddy had placed the ad. Heza could understand how he could do *that* for *some* money at least. Even blind Freddy can paint the wall of a house. Oddy hadn't made a final commitment to selling hot and cold takeaway food yet and still needed a regular earn from a job.

Lawsy's mates down his main *kafeneion* pub all agreed that house-painting was a good, tax-free cash money job ...

Lawsy answered that ad. All he'd have to do is dip a brush in paint and just stroke-stroke-stroke, up, down, backwards, forwards, sideways and forget himself. It was useful for a writer to be alone with thoughts.

## Up A Ladder

Up a ladder Hezza could dwell on things like the splendour of the bush and mateship.

He could enjoy some quiet snorts just to himself too. There was always a demand for house-painters in the inner-city. Gentrification and lots of renovation were happening and house-painter was just another word for *writers* or *foreigners* in those days too. The *kafeneion* was just full of cheap wog labour that had to do *something* for a quid even though it preferred idling, sipping coffee, and playing cards.

Oddy had always wanted to be his own boss; he and Hezza clicked, just two guys up a ladder together, side by side, lost in their own thoughts with only a blank wall to stare at. This was just perfect for having yacks.

## Lawsy And Oddy

Lawsy and Oddy weren't that different.

They both had lots of time, time, time on their hands and in their heads. They were both good at stretching the truth as far as the truth could go and still be called the truth. Oddy was better at telling stories though, even though they were always in Greek and Hezza's Greek was almost as bad as Oddy's English. Hezza would finally write them and Oddy was no good at that either.

## Seeing The World

Of the two of them, Oddy was the one who'd seen more of the world, over more time too.

Hezza rarely even made it to the back fence.

Hezza did more of listening, slow translating and re-membering.

Later, when the *back of* the newspaper was reached and translated down the *kafeneion*, Oddy recognised the stories read to him. They had Hezza's name attached rather than both their names at least. In the end though Oddy decided poor, afflicted Hezza was welcome to them if calling them his own gave him any joy. Oddy *was* illiterate after all and couldn't write them down himself.

### Risky Ladder

Oddy and Hezza felt so content with each other, could actually fall asleep up the ladder and fall off their perch, especially if you were Hezza and had just a few again ... which was the case every other waking moment in his life.

Around every lunch Oddy would swivel around on his bum and face his second-in-command. 'Jeez, I could eat a horse,' he'd hint ... or something like that.

Oddy was the one who'd mostly go for the sandwiches ... because he could without bumping into everything on the way. He'd get to the ground down the ladder, find his land-legs again, turn and face the sky from where all the laughter was coming and go and get the sandwiches. Oddy had grown fond of Hezzy who was becoming a bigger vegie by the day. Getting him up and down the ladder was taking more and more time. Oddy would've liked to be able to perform miracles. That was just another sort of god though. At the very least, he could go and get the lunch. Either the other gods knew what they were doing or they jussssssssssst didn't care. I'm sworn to secrecy though.

### Shouldering A Swag

Hezza got tired of the way things were finally and just shouldered his swag one day.

He grew sick of people's kindness.

## Theo And Gallipoli

Theo went to Gallipoli one day like Oddy once had.

He was getting sick of just hearing about it all the time, however fascinating he also found it. The travel agent had been stoked when he sat down and told him where he wanted to go and how much he wanted to spend.

It was a slow morning that morning however much young Arfstrayans were beginning to love to travel and however fashionable going to Gallipoli was becoming to young Arfstrayans ...

The modget was making the words *patriotism* and *patriotic* fashionable. Theo was going to Greece or what Mama called *back home*. He popped over to Turkey or anti-Greece for a quick look-see and tourist-shop and because he needed a holiday ... from what exactly I'm not sure. Turkey and Greece are quite close to each other, geographically and in every other way too. It'd be almost senseless to go all the way over to one and not see the other.

Theo's first stopover was in Queensland in Arfstraya, at the beach there on the Gold Coast, to catch some rays, soak in the sun, a dip in the water and meet girls, girls, girls, the ads on teev and in the newspaper promised.

## Helga Does Queensland

At the Oh So Tropicana Hotel-Motel Theo suffered his sense of impending doom.

Helga wasn't trying to poison him for his money-belt like he suspected. He'd been warned about the danger of having his money-belt stolen by a greedy foreigner woman by a whole catastrophe of relatives led by Mama that turned up at the airport to see him off. All poor Helga wanted was a holiday romance, some adventure and a quick, exotic grope with a faraway-island kind of stranger at most.

Theo was happy enough at the beginning to imply that he was the one. He *looked* like a Greek. It wasn't Helga poisoning him and it wasn't the fish that they kind of enjoyed together in a tense way at the fish restaurant across the road from the crashing surf that caused his cramps and diarrhoea. He had to spend the entire night on the toe and visited his complimentary ensuite toilet several times. Theo had taken over and ordered for them both. He *was* Arfstrayan and Greek so he double-knew his seafood ... She had to pay for both their meals. She did stifle a yawn politely and smiled her widest smile. It was the tiny octopus hiding in the sand he stepped on as he bashed a noisy way into the surf hoping to impress Helga. He plopped himself down on the sand beside her and flashed her his darkest-eyed look. It usually bowled the ladies over he thought. Pretty, blonde Helga was spread out attractively on the sand in her killer itsy-bitsy, teeny-weeny, tiny teeny, yellow polka-dot bikini. Helga was like most young people. She was like Theo himself in one respect at least. She didn't expect to be around for a long time, just a *good* one.

Theo left their restaurant early. His tummy had started roiling. Mama got a sudden surprise phone call then. She got eighteen actually, one after the other, all reverse-charges. She usually paid the entire phone bill anyway. She'd been asleep. Her dream-life and her daily one were in the same language.

*Dying*

'Of course you'll die!' she screamed at him.

She crossed herself in the Greek Orthodox way, from right to left, from right to left, from right to left.

'We'll all die one day thanks to our maker!' she assured him, letting out a deep breath.

She was a bit annoyed with him. He'd woken her up from a nice dream!

'Why are you going to Turkey?' she demanded when she'd woken up a bit.

### Who Or What Is A Helga?

Lazy Theo presumed Helga was Swedish because she was blonde.

Maybe her ancestors once were ...

### Helga Was A Yank

Helga's a Yank taking a holiday down under though.

Yanks love Arfstraya.

It's just like home, only cheaper. Arfstrayans look at Bali that way and they just love a tourist, especially a Yankee one with Yankee dollars. Tourists are the perfect visitor, only in Arfstraya long enough to spend those dollars and then they go.

Theo worked on Helga for as long as he reckoned it might take to get her out of her smart, red Capri pants. She zipped off back home to her smoggy little apartment in New York, New York, the bossy un-official capital of the US of A as soon as possible. An Arfstrayan from sunny, wide open, spaces might find her apartment a bit tiny and dark, in the shadow of the Twin Towers as it temporarily was. Talk about coincidence. Attaboy was on his knees praying or talking at the sky at *exactly* the same time Osama was ...

If *you* ever need to talk to a god yourself though, you just get yourself down to the pub and find me.

### Creative People

Helga liked to go places where other creative people liked

to go too.

She was quite interested in the arts, in promotion or owning and running an art gallery or something, something creative and worth money too. New York, the kind of centre of the US of A and therefore the world, was just full of creative people running an art gallery or forging a career in fashion or publishing or something at least half-creative.

## Cissy

As well as Helga, Theo met Cissy overseas.

He met her on the magical island of Tourista, one of the sunny islands in the Aegean where he swam in ice-blue water after he ate tourist crab and got warm in the sun. He enjoyed two or three or four or more palate-cleansing ales at the local tourist pub, Ye Olde Swordfish and Fetta over a lonely swordfish and fetta salad *for two* he ordered for him and a *blonde, female* companion hoping to impress her. The food was just an excuse for another drink anyway.

## Swedish Girl

Theo thought that he'd finally scored one of those legendary Swedish girls.

They yack-yack-yacked a while and then drank-drank-drank, there was some eye-eye-eye then, some kiss-kiss-kiss and then they both went back to *her* hotel. Dark Theo was always attracted to whatever he wasn't.

Do you remember what kissing was like after a couple of drinks, all wet and long and messy?

'My name's Circe,' Theo's latest conquest told him. She turned out not to be Swedish but Theo didn't really care. He was getting enough of what he wanted. He got busy covering her fine, blonde legs with kisses but she got sick of him soon. He really only wanted to talk about himself. It was while he was telling her about himself that he told her about old Odysseus. He hoped to impress her with just what an interesting person he was.

'All men are pigs!' Circe hissed at Theo eventually, trying to frighten. Theo just ignored her though. He was too busy talking about himself. Circe threw him one of her dark eyes.

She went silent to show him how to do it and check him out too ... He wasn't too bad-looking she decided with his thick, black eyes, his brown, brown skin and his muscles on muscles. She'd listened in a strangely intent way when he mentioned Oddy's story even if the story was really all about him. Cissy's eyes almost made him pause.

'You could get lost in those snaky curls,' he told himself. Theo ran his hand up and down her firm arm.
'Say hello to Odysseus for me,' Circe hissed at him. 'Tell him Circe says hello.'

'What's that name?' Theo asked, looking up at her just then, his head in her lap while she sat with her legs crossed on her big, white Greek island of a bed. He pecked at her fragrant thigh and looked up. He got a sudden shock!

He was looking up into a sharp, old crone's face.

'Cissy?' his voice quivered.

'Circe,' she corrected him.

Old doe-eyed, dewy-eyed Circe's magic eyes had been working spells for ages showing young men that they were just slaves to the thingummy-jig thing between their legs and the sound of their own voice ...

Circe knew just how to lower her eyes and flutter her lashes seductively like butterflies. She'd been melting rocks with those eyes for ages. She usually showed some lash then.

*Evening Falls Late*
Evening always falls late on well-lit tourists' islands in the

126

Aegean.

Later that night, one uniformed clerk on the front desk of the tourist hotel turned to his mate as Theo ran crazily into the busy, island street.

'Circe must be back from Majorca,' he smiled.

### Theo Finally Does Gallipoli
Jingoists like the modget say that Arfstraya was actually born at noisy Gallipoli.

Arfstraya's Arborigines know too well if anything that that Arfstraya was already born.

### Not That Far
Ithaca from where Theo's folks came from isn't far from Gallipoli.

He popped over there for a look-see before all the hard yakka of going home to Greece. He bought his Mum a phony turquoise necklace at Çanakkale in Turkey just across the strait as a pressie. Arfstrayan tourists buy their ferry and bus tickets to the big G at Çanakkale ... Theo bought a takeaway fish in bread wrap with some tomato, lettuce and white stuff there as well. This was a mistake. Maybe Arfstraya had made him a bit neurotic about fresh food but he thought it smelt ... *fishy* so he tossed into the bin. Food was definitely more plentiful in Arfstraya. Turkish locals saw him do this and looked a bit aghast. Theo just ignored them.

### The Special Link
The modget claims that there's a special link between Arfstraya and Gallipoli.

Lots of young Arfstrayans died there which isn't that difficult to comprehend really. They *were* invading. Gallipoli was in *another* country.

Arfstrayans get really sad every year on Gallipoli Day

or *Anzac* Day or whatever. They cry into beers at a pub somewhere. The word *Anzac* is a very Arfstrayan word. In Çanakkale, Turkey near Gallipoli everything's Anzac. The tourist dollar's very popular there. Theo stayed at The Anzac Hotel, he ate badly at The Anzac Café, drank too much at The Anzac Pub where dry, lonely Arfstrayans with a dollar still left to spend go ... Theo wasn't backward acting out certain national clichés. He was quite happy to buy beers.

## Magic

Theo thought the trip was *magic.*

He didn't yet know that all trips overseas are magic.

Theo's ace American Winged Victory runners were stolen from beside his bed and next morning a mobile phone he'd never seen before sat there instead. He rang his Mum on it.

He went to pay through his nose or his Mama's nose rather for *Anzac* events and tours. He paid for a ticket to the Anzac Dawn Ceremony among other Anzac things at the Anzac Tourist Service in Çanakkale, a sort of one-stop shop. He bought a ticket for The Touch A Little Sheep Tour on which he held a cuddly, newborn lamb in his arms and was introduced to its owner, Gun, an authentic Turk who wasn't too keen on seeing his property in the arms of a wallet on legs.

'This lamb,' Gun insisted, 'this lamb is *my* lamb.'

He looked across to the green, green hills around him sloping gently and to wipe his eyes with his hanky. Gun reminded Theo of his father. His Dad was a peasant once too. Theo came from a peasant *and* an ethnic background.

## Lunch

Lunch that day was a yummy Lamb Tajine in a subtle garlic

sauce. Next on that day's agenda was The Slice of Peasant Bread Dipped In Olive Oil With Goat's Cheese, Red Tomato And Black, Juicy Olives Breakfast. Theo skipped the Buddies Tour even though he'd already paid for it but it sounded just *too* gay. He went on the Blood 'n Bone Tour instead. The battlefield chosen for that year's tour was Suvla Bay where no Arfstrayans actually fell. Theo did though clambering up the hill. Theo misheard. He'd heard *Souvlaki* Bay. He tripped on a bit of old shell casing poking out of the ground there and skinned his shin. Finally came The Dawn Ceremony on the big day on the beach.

'Lousy surf,' thought Theo pretending that he actually knew what good surf looked like. Theo's current fantasy was that he was a toasted, beach-loving Arfstrayan …

He got out of bed early for the ceremony. He still yawned. Getting up this early back home usually meant that there'd been some sort of disaster, a car accident or someone's sister's home late from the movies she'd gone to with girlfriends, boys being off-limits.

Theo had organised a complimentary knock on the door on the morning of the big day from the hotel management who knew what a big day it was for their Arfstrayans. Theo had been as as snug as the proverbial bug in bed. He'd always claimed that he didn't snore.

Most of the others at the Anzac ceremony were older, bleary-eyed guys with their hair parted sharp down the middle. Their permed wives stood next to them in pearls and pink cardies with white feather doonas around their shoulders. People there, including youngsters even younger than Theo wore warm Arfstrayan flags wrapped around their shoulders, keener to show off their patriotism.

Theo's yawn itself was cold. It smoked.

## Delicious

Theo had always found yawning in the morning delicious.

He yawned and stretched his arms out wide. Looking around at Lone Pine, Theo thought about all those old alkies down the *Arms of Britain* with their brown, brown speeches about Vietnam fighting the King Kong. They were lost in the today of things now just like *his* old man had been. Theo could only be impressed by the size of the number of Arfstrayans, New Zealanders, Brits and others who died at Gallipoli, not even to mention the number of Turks. Theo bounced and bounced his nervous sneaker against the stone wall around the official cemetery, Ari Burnu. There were so many white crosses there all Theo could do is stop counting and feel sort of lonely instead. The idea of all that courage blew him out. The scent of the local thyme he absent-mindedly tickled under his nose with was like the aromatic scent of a gum leaf.

## Oi

There was a moment when Theo pushed off the wall with a new sneaker, ready to bolt.

A drunken yob started chanting.

He chanted *oi, oi, oi*. Theo presumed that he hated wogs. Hoons often did.

He wore a striped black, white, brown, yellow and green footy jumper, matching woollen scarf and beanie. He was a very drunk and loud supporter despite being at a solemn ceremony of remembrance rather than a footy match. The younger blokes all urged him on.

'Arssie, Arssie, Arssie, oi, oi, oi,' he chanted. 'Oogie oogie oogie!'

An old bloke finally walked over angrily and dropped a picnic blanket over his head. Theo started crab-crab-crab-bing sideways, sideways, sideways down the wall.

### Kostas
Kostas owned the Çanakkale pensione where Theo stayed.

He couldn't accept that brown Theo wasn't a Greek. He mostly wore black. Theo insisted that he wasn't though, that he was an Arfstralo. Kostas wondered whether Theo meant Englishman.

He did wonder how Theo could be Greek and English at the same time.

Kostas wasn't the sharpest tool in the box. He was kind though. He kept an eye on Theo for his Mama's sake and he hadn't even been asked to. If Theo wasn't English and he wasn't Greek, he wondered, then what was he? *Oudeis?* Oddy? Nobody?

### Home
Theo had always felt a bit lost.

If Greece was home and Arstraya was home, did that mean he had two homes?

Theo's folks had went to a lot of trouble to leave their sunny homes to come to a sunny country with a future.

They'd had enough of poverty, hunger and war.

### Back Home
Theo was glad to get back home where he could run with his Boys and fight in the streetss.

His Boys would be glad to be see him ... he hoped.

He would certainly be glad to see them at last. He looked forward to a welcome back hit in the arm. Overseas was not good for scoring. He didn't know his way around somewhere else. Theo looked forward to the busy streets of home he just knew.

He looked forward to gettings sleepy again just like in

old times. Theo liked the world being predictable even if that meant the rich would just get richer and the poor poorer.

### Oddy Gets Goes Where He Was Going

Oddy travelled the length of the city one tired summer's morning to get where he was going.

The whole trip involved getting one bus and two trams.

He'd always found staring Arfstrayans a bit rude. Oddy stared back but history just doesn't say whether anyone noticed. The tram conductor pretended he couldn't understand his broken English and just ignored him. Oddy just patted his wiry, springy hair down, shaped his mustache and perched his hat on things.

There was a stiff breeze blowing that day.

### Unfriendly Arfstrayans

Oddy took a deep breath.

He still had of the rest of his life to go. There was still a fair way to go on the crowded tram. It wasn't that easy to get to the exit in the crush. He angled and angled his way towards it.

''Scuse, 'scuse, 'scuse,' he 'scused himself. He was growing flustered under his felt hat. He'd learned a while ago that the only way forward was forward. He was heading to the big Town Hall in town to pay good money for a *hot* takeaway food vendor's licence. Oddy was growing sick of having to avoid coppers all the time.

### Oddy Got Depressed

Oddy couldn't stop himself getting depressed.

He feared all the young spirited fellers were heading to the Town Hall too for *their* food vendor's licence. He found himself wondering how he could make a living with all these other food vendors around too.

'This a-way, this a-way?' they all laughed and mocked him.

Oddy found himsef wondering nervously like he often did almost obsessively if they were laughing at him because he was a gyppo. He couldn't do anything about his foreign looks. He'd got them from his sainted Mama who was a ghost now.

He perspired. He didn't sweat. Only animals sweat. He might be a gyppo, but he wasn't an animal. He wanted some official permission though.

*Oddy Was A Little Man*

Oddy wasn't ever a big man.

He just got old.

This lot weren't bad Boys, they were just loud and a bit boisterous. They weren't even close to being a mob. This was just a crowd of fifteen, sixteen or seventeen year-old Boys almost groaning with boredom.

'Here, gyppo, here, mate, over here,' they chanted … affectionately.

Oddy smiled and smiled back. He found that he understood one word at least.

'It's gonna be a lark!' they grinned at him.

Oddy had once eaten a lark someone had shot.

These Boys lot were just Boys being Boys. They were just mocking people who almost demanded to be mocked. Oddy had encountered worse outside pubs. This was only like a sporting fixture crowd or any other mob of hungry punters with good cash-money.

'Hot doggy, doggy, doggy, *yeeros, yeeros, yeeros!*' he chanted.

'Here, here, here,' The Boys chanted back and sent him up.

'Hurry, *mate*, hurry! It'll all be over before we even get there.'

## The Sadness Of Odysseus

Never mind what his face said, Oddy wasn't feeling scared.

He was just feeling sad.

All these innocent, ignorant Boys were going to die one day soon. He could actually see that. He was always quite farsighted as gods went. He could see that the Arfstrayan Boys were the tallest, the best-fed, the best-looking, the funniest, the fastest, the toughest, the fairest, the most everything Boys that ever were and they were from the best gods' own country in the world. All the superlatives were making Oddy feel *most* giddy. The sun that day was quite probably the hottest ever.

Oddy had only just learnt that there was a war on down the *kafeneion* when an out-of-date newspaper was read out aloud to everybody there by Oddy's best coffee-crony. The coffee and the world conflict had both been brewing and whistling for ages. Escaping conscription amongst heathen Turks was the major reason Oddy and many of his *kafeneion* buddies left home and migrated and now enjoyed tiny, tasty little cups of coffee in safe, distant Arfstraya. All Oddy needed now was a hot food-vendor's licence.

## Too Much

Far too much of Oddy's money since he came to Arfstraya had been spent paying off cops.

He resented having to fork money out just so he could be left alone in his hot woollen suit in the sun just so he could work hard. Oddy got into his first ever bad mood.

Oddy could sign his own name if he had to, but he was basically illiterate. He needed help from some kind stranger ... who weren't all that easy to find in Arfstraya if you were a gyppo ... to do all the rest. There was a big poster of some angry bearded guy in a uniform like some copper's outside The Town Hall pointing rudely into your face and screaming, 'You!'

## Drowning

Oddy was just about drowning in a sea of *sad*.

He finally made it through the Town Hall's big double doors. There was a big oaf in another uniform sitting at a desk just inside where Oddy could apply for his food-vendor's licence.

'Everybody in Arfstraya likes wearing a uniform, even the clerks,' Oddy thought to himself as he stood before him. Being a copper in Arfstraya had always been at least better than being a convict ...

The uniformed bulldog's bark made Oddy dance from one foot to the other like a little boy waiting for ages to get into the Little Mens'.

'You gonna stand there all day with that silly, gyppo look on yer face then?' The oaf's rubbery face shook at Oddy.

'C'mon, c'mon,' he bellowed! 'What's yer name?'

The uniformed boof's thick neck had turned a dangerous purple like he was exploding.

'Carve 'er up, mate!' he bellowed when Oddy tried his real name on him.

'Yer name's too bloody long!'

This was when Oddy lost his old surname and got the new name, Carver.

He got the new first name, Private too.

## Click, Clock

Time passed slowly and loudly.

Oddy could hear the divine clock ticking on.

He realised too then that the oaf was scratching the

wrong name onto his page.

The bully even barked in his f-ing oath of a language on the page.

'*Ochi*,' he blurted! As usual Oddy didn't know how to say what he wanted to ...

The surprised oaf tap-tap-taped his pen's nib on his desk and waited for something that would never come.

## Bloody Long Day

It had already been a long day.

Luckily, Oddy had started it off with a solid breakfast of eggs and toast in the morning. Oddy had learnt that burnt bread was called toast in Arfstraya.

Oddy hadn't invented the toaster yet.

He was enjoying olives and a sliced onion with a glass of water rather than the table wine or raki he used to enjoy too. He had some boiled oats too or porridge as it was called. Odd thought once that only the horses that he usually lost money on when they were racing had oats. He wasn't a gyppo and he wasn't an animal either.

He just wanted a *legal* licence.

He would've liked to stop stuttering too when he was being hassled by coppers.

'Next!' roared the bully, telling Oddy know he was over now and that he should be making room for the blond boy next in line. The bully wanted to bark at someone new now in his f-ing oath of a language.

## What Oddy Knew

The next thing Oddy knew he was climbed briskly into a bunk on a ship on water.

He was glad to be lying down. It had been such a long, tiring day. It started early when Oddy untangled himself from the arms of his latest boarding-house widow.

He really wanted that *official* licence. The coppers' grins were beginning to insist that Arfstraya wasn't his country.

Untidy sleeping sounds were coming from the bunks around him full of exhausted Boys sleeping badly. Oddy just had to fall asleep to dream and start understanding. Morning arrived eventually. Another uniformed bully came with it and started barking.

Oddy woke with a start. He was in a narrow bunk of a spot *again*. It was still gloomy outside. All the chugging told him that the ship had left the dock and was heading wherever it was going. Oddy was on the HMAS *Sydney* or the HMAS *Melbourne* or the HMAS *Brisbane* or the HMAS *Adelaide* or the HMAS *Perth* or the HMAS *Hobart* or somewhere capital. I only know for sure that it wasn't the HMAS *Darwin* or the HMAS *Canberra*. Oddy hadn't founded those places yet.

Young and still enthusiastic Boys jumped out of their bunks immediately with all the eagerness of youth and started punching each other in the arm to show just how much they liked each other. Oddy got punched a lot just to show how popular he already was even though he was older and different. Oddy's sadness just grew more. The ship's up and down comforted him just like his Mama's rocking arms used to when he was a baby. The scratchy new khaki uniform bothered him. Oddy had lots of questions too like whether all official hot food vendors in Arfstraya had to wear uniforms like this and why did hot food vendors' school have to be overseas and why exactly did he have to have a different name?

## Odysseus Confused

All the daily little bouts of xenophobia Oddy experienced in Afstraya confused him.

It wasn't the presence of hostility as such. It was the absence of the *filoxenia* he'd learnt all about back on Ithaca in his Mama's lap when he was still a little kid. *Filoxenia* was otherwise known as the love of strangers. *Filoxenia* could be just a smile from some stranger in the street who might just be another god.

Arfstraya didn't feel all that strange to Odysseus, probably because it was an island *girt by sea* like magical Ithaca was where he'd grown up happily in the groves of scented pines and olive groves where dryads live. He ended up in better everything Arfstraya where a fortune can be made if you're a hard-working migrant.

*Foreign Countries*

The past *is* such a foreign country.

It's always being left behind.

The future's another one that people can only hope they get to eventually. The present can feel pretty strange too sometimes.

We're just interested in the past in this story though.

*New Friends*

Oddy made a lot of new friends on the ship chuffing slowly to Gyppoland.

There was Mr Bluey, Messieurs Red, Big and Little, Mr White, Mr Jacko and all the other misters he couldn't recall when he was telling Theo about them.

Oddy had more friends than he usually had and they liked him too. He could tell by the number of times they biffed him in the arm like comrades sometims do and then smiled at him. His new friends gave him another new name. Oddy became known as Old Black'n'Tan. His age and colour scheme, oily black on top and brown everywhere else was what the name referred to. Oddy insisted on being addressed as *Mr* Black'n'Tan though. He always simply demanded respect.

He was also called Gypp sometimes ... or *Mr* Gypp rather

*Good On Ya*

'Good on ya, *Mr* Gypp!' one of the Boys would yell, thump him hard in the arm and grin.

Being Oddy was becoming a bit painful. He was *the* elder on the ship. He expected respect and to be left alone. The Boys were younger and just had more energy than he did. He was usually fast asleep and snoring as The Boys raged around him, punching each other in the arm and wrestling when it was lights-out time. His head would hit his hessian pillow at the end of the day with relief. The Boys were still young, Oddy used to remind himself a lot. He wasn't in the full bloom of youthful anything anymore. He *needed* his sleep. The finest, imported white cotton pillows usually went straight to the officers who were mostly older men like him. Oddy wasn't exactly sure why he hadn't been made an officer. He considered the possibility of the racism he was learning to expect.

He smiled at the officers he saw as just like him. A lot of them looked like they might be as old as he was but they never smiled back. They scowled at him or looked away instead. What really confused him though was how Arfstrayan officers dressed just like their inferiors with just an additional ribbon or two the difference. Oddy found Arfstrayan egalitarianism dishonest. An officer was still an officer whatever he wore like a copper was still a copper whether *he* wore a uniform or not. Oddy often found himself being barked at by some pup half his age wearing more ribbons than Oddy knew existed. Oddy had always worked off the idea that if it looked like a duck and quacked, then it was probably a duck. The *appearance* of egalitarianism in Arfstraya wasn't always the same as all things being equal though.

A good example of just how much an Arfstrayan officer could confuse an issue was Major General Julius Caesar Pompy Augustus King William George the Fourth. His Boys just loved him. That's Major General Julius Caesar Pompy Augustus King William George and *not* General Major Julius Caesar Pompy Augustus King William George. This is the guy his men fondly knew as Old Pomp'n'Circumstance. He wasn't a bad old stick as old sticks went. Officer material could be nob material but old Pomp was an Arfstrayan officer-nob so he was just like one of his inferiors. Oddy used to go the full hog. He seemed to insist on jumping up to attention, clicking his heels and saluting if there was an officer even in the vicinity. Oddy jumped and saluted even when the officer was still quite far away ... Oddy saluted and saluted at old Pomp so much whenever he came down below decks that Pomp presumed that Oddy might be sending him up. He ordered Oddy to please stop clicking his heels and saluting so much ... He had to have Oddy thrown into the ship's brig to get him to stop. Some Arfstrayan officers were worse than others though. One of them apparently ticked off one of the wounded for not *lying* at attention sternly enough in bed.

*There Was One Thing*
Something the nobs used to do sometimes grabbed Oddy's attention.

The one-eyed monocle thing impressed him a good deal. He was grabbed by the effort they were simply to put into holding a *glass* eye in your real one with just that real eye itself.

## The Point

All by himself Oddy couldn't see, not with both eyes open.

Was it all about being superior or was just sheer affectation talking?

The glare in a sunny place like Arfstraya made him wonder. He also wondered why there the other eye shouldn't have a monocle too.

This was when Oddy arrived at one of his most lucrative ideas. He invented sunglasses, so to speak, the simple idea of *two* dark monocles and not just one.

## Things In Writing

Oddy forgot to put anything in writing *again*.

He couldn't write anyway ...

Optical goods manufacturers have been making wads of money for a while.

It could've all been Oddy's, *if* he'd been able to write. School kids should be paying attention to that ... There's not too much point in being rich in Hades though ...

## As Big And Brave

'Arfstrayan officers are just as big and brave as anyone else's,' Oddy insisted to Theo.

They could yell just as loud and make their men jump up, down or sideways or in any direction they wanted them to, even through a hula hoop if necessary, ruggedly like an Arfstrayan would, tugging a forelock.

Oddy couldn't work out why Arfstrayan officers had to yell so much in ruling class British accents though.

They did sound a bit strange from Arfstrayan mouths. They sounded silly enough coming out of British ones.

Oddy just supposed that Britain, mother of all officers ... or British Accent Land as it was also known ... must've been full of toffee accents.

Wherever it came from, it hurt his ear. Oddy wished that it could just go back there soon. A British accent was going to be the main sound of the next khaki while.

*Now!*
'Get up to the deck *now* for parade!'

Loud orders in faux-British accents when he was almost asleep were becoming the norm. A chilly shadow was just beginning to fall over the innocent playground of a mind Oddy played in. He wanted sleep to come now from just around the corner where they waited despite the smelly, lumpy pillows everyone had to lay a worn-out head on.

*Lucky Oddy*
Oddy and Fate collided upstairs where everyone was marched from stale, oily downstairs in the morning for some fresh air and sunshine and given a run around the ship ...

Fate struck Oddy in the head not just *once* ... but *twice*. *Two* birds fell into his head. The gods know that one out of one huge sky in one world into one head is lucky enough. It's as rare as finding just the one in a bush. I think that maybe Oddy's relatives were involved.

The first time it happened the bird was dead and just fell out of the sky. Oddy staggered around dazed a bit, more confused than usual even, his head all concentric circle. Officers yelled pointlessly because they weren't really sure what else they could do ... Oddy wondered whether *this* was the lark The Boys outside The Town Hall talked about when he came to, blink-blink-blinked and stumble-stumble-stumbled around. All his new mates lined up to biff him in the arm again. They'd have a turn and cut straight back to the end of the line for another one. They were so fond of him. There were blokes taking a turn Oddy had never seen before. Oddy burst into tears. He was so moved, I suppose. The second time it happened, the big, noisy bird landing on his head was still alive and holding an olive branch in its beak.

## Able To Read
Oddy could've read about this if he'd been able to read.

He knew from his seafaring days though that this meant landfall was close.

The bird just wasn't sure of its footing on this slippery, screaming rock so it dug its uncertain claws in ... Oddy ran around and around in noisy circles, wearing a squawking lady's hat. His comrades all lined up and bunching fists threw their diggers' hats at his loud head again. By the time Oddy finished his time on the ship, he was wonkier but he'd never felt so loved in all his life.

## Soon
They arrived where they were going soon.

They rowed ashore in long, wooden boats, officers screaming in clipped, faux-British accents again.

When he finally got where he'd always been heading, Oddy found himself standing on shifting desert sands.

He was in Gyppoland.

The trenches were coming soon, their holes in the ground, their practice graves where officers were always screaming again, to make them feel right at home. Oddy did more jumping into holes and out again than he ever thought he'd do. A clipped British accent could make an Arfstrayan jump quite high it seemed.

## The Shining Sun
The sun was shining.

One of the Boys in Oddy's boat had tied a bootlace over his hat so it wouldn't go flying in the breeze. He looked like a big dag. His name was Chicka and his oars worked hard like everyone else's did. The boat whistled along. Everything almost was blue, the water under them and the sky above.

The day was perfect for gods and mortals too. Chicka was poised to spring ashore like a cat as soon as the boat ground there. Whoom, whoom, whoom! The sea itself was exploding and showering soaking water all over them.

Officers yelled orders like they were yelling orders in a fish-shop down the road from the pub after closing at home. Seagulls caw-cawed and the mates all sat up hard over their oars and just stared. If they weren't Arfstrayans, they would probably have got more scared

The shells were just practice duds though. The rifles were all loaded with blanks too ... Their officers' pistols were loaded with live ammo though.

The authorities there too were all too-aware of the possibility of mutiny ... That says a lot about just how popular their idea of adventure was, doesn't it?

*Wet Behind The Ears*
Naturally the Arfstrayan Boys got wet.

They got so frightened when duds started crumping around them that they wet themselves.

When they realised the explosions were mostly just sound rather than fury they started laughing and giggling like thoughtless gods.

Some of The Boys had headaches from the night before. Oddy certainly did.

The others had surrounded him and made him chug-a-lug beer until he passed out.

It was the day after now and their boat cut through the waves and headed forward, forward and ever onward, faster, faster and faster until it bounce-bounce-bounced into the beach, scrape-scrape-scraping ashore. The Boys jumped out of their boats … led by Oddy. They settled into orderly lines ashore, each man shoulder to shoulder next to the mate next door, arm's length-arm's length-arms length, digger's hats cocked and jaunty, rifles shouldered and officers still screaming and yelling.

## Gyppos

Gyppos swarmed all over The Boys while they just stood there at attention.

Gyppos wearing stripy tents yelled out their wares and prices.

They just about climbed all over The Boys to get their attention. They shouted *Inglisz, Inglisz, Inglisz* at them in a messy, overseas way.

Nobody knew … Was *blah blah blah piastres* a good price for doughnuts, oranges and all the other probably quite unhygienic junk on sale? Oddy had to stand at attention for a long, hot, panting time. All the while officers glared and circled, whacking their legs with their riding-crops.

This world's aromas and sounds were only as strange to Oddy as Arfstrayan ones once were. Oddy was a Gypp too or half-a-Gypp at least and half a god.

Half a Gypp was more than enough Gypp for many Arfstrayans. It wasn't always felt that Oddy was enough of a white man anyway, whatever fraction he was supposed to be.

Arfstrayan army officers weren't any more stupid or cruel than anyone else's. The Boys just had to stand there in silence and not break ranks for a little while. All they needed was water-water-water. They wilted finally and dropped in the sand just where they stood. Oddy was already used to the sun and screaming Gyppos.

He could've taught the others a thing or two about haggling. It was just a game, after all like two-up or boxing. He could've taught the hawkers a thing or two too like how to tone themselves down a bit if they hoped to sell anything to Arfstrayans who didn't know just what they wanted. Oddy just wanted the officers to stop barking at him.

*Cairo Stinks*
Cairo stinks.

It used to back then too.
Old Cairo *can* get a bit smoky.

Its cooking fires alone used to make for a thick, permanent, smoky cloud.

The Arfstrayan Boys showed very little curiosity about any place that wasn't home. They just weren't very good travellers like Oddy was. He had aeons and aeons of practice though. He wasn't as insistently unworldly as they were.

I think that maybe The Arfstrayan Boys still needed their Mamas and the spanking on their bottoms that she used to give them.

*O Woe*
The very idea of Arfstrayan Boys in a place as old as Cairo can give me the pip.

It was *not*-Arfstraya. It was full of black people who were still alive.

Oddy coughed and sneezed like visitors often do ...
Smog's such a modern world thing.

Oddy could've told them that there were worse things than smog ... There's death for instance ... Even Hades isn't entirely free of smoke, not with all those fires raging around it. Life's not everything though. You'd think that this would be the type of motto that would be very popular on Hades T-shirts and posters.

I'm not sure if there's a Hades travel package or travel

agent or travel something though.

I would've made a great entrepreneur I think.

### Foreign Everything

The Boys had already been frightened by all the loud, foreign gestures in the place.

Arfstrayans in the old days were a bit provincial *wherever* they went. As well they were young Boys and they'd been penned up for just too long learning how to kill, be killed and such things. Things were just like once upon a time when they were little kids. They felt like there was nothing to lose if they behaved badly ... and so they did ... They were just showing off a bit that they were The Boys from the Third Battalion of the Arfstrayan Imperial Forces or AIF. High Command decided The Boys should have some distraction before *life* in the trenches ... which was at least better than *death* in the trenches and just let them loose in the Wazza, poor Cairo's red-light district which was just full of cheap booze, cheap women and cheap thrills. The Arfstrayan Boys went all no-bloody-worries or Arssie, Arssie, Arssie, oi, oi, oi or something and acted like little little children who were let off the leash. The main event was just around the corner. The Boys worried that maybe the bloody foreigners or Arabs or whoever they were only interested in them for their pounds, shillings and pence. They were right too.

### Dead

There was one officer who would stop anyone dead. He was a real Cyclops of a man with a monocle screwed into his face and it shone in the sun. The Boys had to get right out of his barking way as he marched crisply towards the souk, scattering gyppos and all lesser mortals before him. He whacked and whacked his leg with a leather riding-crop as he marched. At one needle of a moment, he turned his head

woodenly and fixed Oddy on the spot with his glaring sun
of an eye. The Boys yahooed and hooted mocked all around
him and scattered if he turned on them. Arfstrayans can be
so disrespectful to authority ... *up to a point.*

## Away From Home

Oddy was away from home where he knew no one and no
one knew him.

He was all cashed up with no girlfriend to go out with,
so to speak. A man does gotta do what a man's gotta do
even if he's only half a man ... This *was* The Wazza. There
were part-time girlfriends everywhere tugging at drunken
khaki elbows.

Oddy stopped in front of one tent-y wench displaying her
wares in a doorway. The woman burst out laughing at him.
Poor Oddy just laughed back. He thought that this might be
the polite thing to do. The surprised woman started screaming at him then though.

Shush-shushing her and trying to get her to keep it down
just made her scream more. What precisely she was screaming at Oddy just doesn't bear repeating ... almost.

## She Screamed

She screamed that there were five hungry kids to feed back
home, not to mention a hungry husband called Browny who
was about the same colour as Oddy to put oats or couscous
or something on the table for. The fleet was in and the ill-lit
lanes were full of rich white Boys and their officer Daddies
... or wallets on legs ... and now here was fuckin', un-fucka-
ble Oddy who was almost as black and dark as she was. He
wanted to spill some whatever ... some oats and waste her
time at *her* expense.

'Get lost! Go on, go away, she cried! My husband's whiter than you are and his name's Browny!'

That's as much of what she had to say to Oddy as Oddy just got confused *again*. He was the same colour as he'd always been!

'Wog-fight, wog-fight, wog-fight!' they chanted.

*Frozen Again!*

Odd came close to tears.

'Here, big Daddy, here, here!' the tent-y wench went back to chanting with all the other wenches, their attention more back usefully to Arfstrayans staggering by as drunk as lords.

*The Flying Piano*

Pianos fly.

Sofas and heavy hand-carved tables did too. The more rare things were, the more they flew. Arfstraya's youngest, bravest and finest had broken out of The Wazza where they had been corralled by their optimistic officers. The Boys learned that poor neighbourhoods weren't nearly as much fun as rich ones that night and that poor neighbourhoods burn better. The Boys also learned that there were different kinds of Gyppo. They learnt this when Gypp sprinters fled their burning hearths and homes, screaming and yelling in French Gypp, Italian Gypp, Greek Gypp, English Gypp and even in Turkish Gypp ... Greek wails in particular brought Oddy's head up.

The Boys didn't realise at the time that there were people they saw that night who they'd see again back in Arfstraya one day in milk bars, cafés, factories and driving hansom taxis. That night is known now as The Battle of the Wazza. Arborigines often found out how horrible it could be when white Arfstrayan Boys looked for what they could get ...

149

*Discipline*

After The Night of The Wazza, The Boys were marched back to barracks in the desert with their headaches and emptied wallets and just went back to day-long marches and being told what to do. They were told to jump in and out of holes in the ground or storming other holes full of pretend-Turks.

They stormed these trenches repeatedly under the eternal eye of the Sphinx described by The Boys as wearing a face like a kangaroo that's been punched in the head. The Pyramids were described as piles of wombat-poo, even though most of them had never even seen a wombat outside a zoo or a kangaroo or an old-man emu or anything wild, free and Arfstrayan.

*Ignorance And Stupidity*

Ignorance and stupidity look just like each other sometimes.

*Yet Another Very Hot Day*

The Boys went by hasty lifeboat from their swaying ship across the smoking, exploding sea to land that was exploding too. Bombs whistled as they fell and landed with a crump. No amount of training could've ever prepared them for the salty spume and watery fume. The sea itself boomed.

*The National War Museum*

There's one of those old boats hanging up in The National War Museum.

There was a sign hanging next to it.

*Burrowing*

This one poor bloke I heard about burrowed deep into the bottom of his boat, trying to just get away somehow. Bullets flew around him.

Maybe you can see why I became a bloodthirsty god. I just went with the way things are.

## The Museum Some More

I went to the Museum some more to see if I could find a photo there of this bloke I knew.

We used to have a beer together and tell each other a few lies … have a conversation, I mean.

Sometimes I'm glad I'm a god and not just another stupid person.

## Boom, Boom, Boom

Oddy looked away at one point when he was crawling up the hill at Kum Kale.

There was a particularly mad bombardment going on. Oddy and The Boys had just been dropped nowhere and *up* was the only way to go. It was so loud out there that Oddy kept only one eye open at a time. He had to keep the other one shut. He was blinded by the screaming, crying and the glare after glare of light. He was full of a feeling that he'd been here before …

He had.

It was during that big Trojan War thing, the other big slaughter in his life before death. There'd been less flying metal around the first time. Oddy's old mate, messy Achilles was there, leaving torn corpses lying around all over the place, here, there, wherever …

## Loudness

The blinding loudness of the day kept coming back to him all Oddy's life.

Things used to get pretty loud when he was kissing Beryl on her full mouth or on the inside of one of her white, white luscious thighs. He hadn't been able to believe he was there either. There was a pair of white, white legs just standing there smoking at Gallipoli too. They once belonged to Bluey or Snowy. They'd both liked smoking.

## Chance And Her Twin, Luck

Oddy was once very fond of the goddess, Chance and Luck too, her twin sister.

Oddy used to like strolling between the two of them on gentle, moonlit nights, a good-time gal on each of his arms.

It eventually dawned on The Boys that a sudden thud in the face could tear out their eyes and leave them flailing and bumping into things for the rest of their bumpy days. Oddy turned whiter than he'd ever gone before. He stopped knowing altogether.

I think that this was when his head was emptied for the rest of his days. Boom, boom, boom, boom, boom. The world turned an all-black nothing or an all-white one or a white and black nothing or a nothing-nothing.

Oddy lost his zing *and* his zang, and learnt that endurance was more important than courage. Sometimes I think that this might have been when he started turning old.

## Trust

Oddy hadn't trusted banks since his Kelly days.

## Doing Well

Some people didn't do that badly thanks to the old man.

I didn't do too bad myself thanks to Theo and Oddy of course.

Oddy's bomb had made him prone to just giving things away. He was discombobulated ... The bomb knocked even the memory out of him. His memories would only come back in the form of dreams. He dreamed about things like the wet, leaking heads cradled in his lap on his stagger down

Kum Kale after his bomb. He was holding an oar in his hands as he climbed down carefully through the crimson, thorny gorse.

He didn't really care anymore though. He'd had enough. The screaming, leaking heads cradled in his lap belonged to some of the best mates Oddy ever had in his ridiculously long life. His memory of the Kum Kale day never went away or the memory of the ripped bodies lying wherever they'd been tossed by the big boom. It was the black Lord Kitchener who sent the Arfstrayans into that mess. It was a wonder frankly that any of them got to see the next day. Oddy almost didn't. The traditions all agree that his bomb sent him flying.

## Oddy Was Very Excited

Oddy grew very excited the last day he was telling Theo his story.

He was getting curried sausages and spaghetti mash for dinner that night and next night was egg'n'salami omelette night. While Oddy was telling him all this, his prettiest nurse couldn't keep her eyes off Theo according to Theo.

He perched himself on the edge of Oddy's bed, as far away from the smelly old man as he could get.

He smooth-smooth-smoothed the old man's top woollen blanket over and over again as he listened to Oddy's fantastic story.

## It Tickled

Oddy giggled.

The flying bullets around him were sounding like so many whining mozzies.

Maybe bombs do tickle. I wouldn't know. Maybe some of the shades down Hades would know for sure.

### Heyamola

It was the Turkish *heyamola* who found Oddy just lying where his bomb blew him.

Oddy was always on another side.

### Seeping Into Consciousness

It slowly seeped into Oddy's consciousness as his eyes slitted open that the whispering going on over him was Turkish whispering and the uniforms standing there were grey and not the khaki like Arfstrayans wore.

The gods have always loved a good joke. We love a bad one too. It just has to be a joke.

The Johnny-Turks climbed slowly down the hill littered with torn, bloody bits of ex-Arfstrayans. The gorse was crimson again just like when Oddy travelled *up* one. They hoped to find treasures that the Arfstrayans left behind when they left suddenly because their latest assault had failed too …

### Oddy's New Mates

Oddy's new best mates didn't kill him because they thought he was one of them.

He *was* the same colour as they were, brown rather than the pasty white the Inglisz madmen were.

The Inglisz madmen had just turned up out of the deep blue ocean and just invaded.

### Hold This

'Here, hold my bloody rifle for me, will you?' Memish grunted at his best mate, Kemal.

### Around The Campfire

Oddy spent much of his next while beside a blazing campfire behind the Turkish trench.

He wanted to fight off the chilly days and even chillier

nights as much as possible. Life in the *heyamola* trench was a bit happier than life in his old trench with the cobbers as just munchy for rats to sharpen their ratty teeth on. A familiar head would sneak unwisely over the edge of the trench opposite from time to time. He had to be seen to be shooting at it by a new trench-mate or get into some big trouble.

There was one particularly tense moment. The umpteenth futile charge by his old mates, The Blue Boys, had just failed. The Arssies were driven over the top by one barking officer or another. Maybe the same uniformed twit or another one with a hairy upper lip would scream them across the mess of blood and bits between the two trenches that was known as No Man's Land. Oddy popped and popped his rifle into the sky, shooting only the odd starling at worst or at the trench opposite and lobbed grenade-bombs until he won his way into *that* trench again and again.

Oddy fought like a madman back and forth between the two trenches, wondering just what the point was sometimes. He used to forget which trench he was supposed to be in sometimes, *ours* or *theirs* ...

After another assault to where he used to be not that long ago, Oddy tripped over the torn body of a dead Arfstrayan Boy as he slithered quickly into the Arssie hole ... The dead Arssie Boy hung there over the lip of the trench, half-in and half-out, his blood drip-drip-dripping down the identity disc hanging arounds his ripped neck.

Oddy had a moment. He wondered if he was the one who shot the messy Boy ... He screamed loudly. Memish slapped him hard on the shoulder like a comrade and rescued him again.

There was another moment too. A mysterious, mad, old Turk creaked himself out of Oddy's current trench and stumble-stumble-stumbled across to the Arssie slit across the way and just stood there. Not a single khaki rifle popped and not a single Arssie bomb lobbed. Arssies threw cans of food at him instead.

Arfstrayan hearts *can* be soft, thank Allah, but then came a bang!

The tiniest peep could've shattered the silence in both the lines.

### Mercy Was Prized

Oddy's new comrades prized mercy.

They'd take a break behind the trench and sip orange-blossom peel tea from a good, solid mug filled from a communal billy sitting on the fire and just chat as often as they could. Oddy went with them and rubbed chilly hands together over the communal fire.

### Life Is For Living

Oddy's *new* Boys showed him that life was for living even in an abattoir.

Oddy had new things to learn wherever he was ...

In the Arfstrayan trench Oddy was introduced to the new-fangled rolly roll-your-own cigarettes. If only he could have understood toasted, old jokes, then things would've been just perfect. Cigarettes, tea, friends, *heyamola* ...

It was clearly a time for new things.

### No Man's Land

Galllipoli was so noisy.

Rifles tap-tap-tapped all the time, bombs lobbed and crumped and shovels scrape-scrape-scraped. The infernal battlefield sounded a bit like old Hephaestos, the divine, lame blacksmith's workshop.

Imagine things just going back to the way things used to be with just the ssh-ssh-shushing of little waves on the beach next door.

Keep imagining. Imagine all the rifles falling silent at the one time.

This *was* unlikely. The two sets of imperial fodder even wore different colours. Arfstrayans wore their khaki and the Turks wore *their* grey. They even used different rifles. The Arfstrayans used Lee Enfields going bang thwack. The Turks liked using German Mausers that went boom thunk. Oddy smoked the communal hookah with his *heyamola* now rather than the other side's individual rolly cigarettes he could only enjoy by himself. Oddy hadn't experienced the *filoxenia* the Turks offered like Greeks. The comradeship amongst his new mates was just like Ithacan *filoxenia*. The only way forward was obviously forward.

Oddy's grey *friends* did all of the talking as he didn't speak Turkish ... He had to pretend he was dumb ... Being dumb was certainly better than being shot.

### Stumble-Stumble-Stumbling

One night Oddy woke and felt an urge.

He stumble-stumbled out of the trench for a quick whatever and discovered that *out there* could be much worse than inside.

He was still half-asleep and looked around. He found himself looking on *just* nothing.

### No Man's Land

Oddy was looking on No Man's Land.

It was full of bloody Arfstrayan, Brit, Kiwi or Johnny shreds and ribbons all looking just the same and equal. Everyone was just the same as each other at Gallipoli. Again the place could be used to teach.

### Trench-mood

Oddy rested his forehead on his arm and tasted trench-mood on both sides.

He learnt how to sigh a lot in two languages hour after long hour.

### A Hole In The Ground

Gallipoli now was full of holes in the ground and people living in them.

He thought a while about how this wasn't a place so much as it was a place between places, just ground between two graves full of breathing people. An anti-place like this turned unbelievers into believers. People here *wanted* to believe in a god. I've always thought it was a good idea. If Oddy had been a mortal, he would probably would have enjoyed the glowing campfire more, just nodding and nodding on at his *heyamola* like he actually understood what they were saying to him, a sprig of something local and aromatic and not unlike that gum-leaf under his nose.

### The Heyamola

'The donkeys the Inglisz use to carry their wounded, they're good donkeys.'

Memish was speaking in his usual slow way. He made one good point after the other with the new-fangled rolly cigarette between his fingers. Oddy had introduced them to his new grey trench-mates ...

Memish used to be a farmer once and raised crops. He used to breed and raise donkeys too. He knew them very well indeed ... There wasn't going to be much more farming or anything in Memish's life soon though. There wasn't going to be much more of a life.

His face was being torn off by a bullet soon. He was in quite good spirits for the moment though, just sitting next to a warm fire and yapping with mates. Wordless Oddy sprawled in the blasted dirt behind the trench with Kemal, Adil and smelly, swarthy Gun. Someone would lean over every now and then, choose a sizzling skewer of roasted meat off the fire, slap it between two pieces of damper Oddy had just made, spoon some of his chopped garlic, wild fennel and hot pepper in a tomato sauce on and hand sandwiches around. The others would just continue yack-yack-yacking and making good point after good point with their smokes, take another bite then and wipe a greasy hand across a bristly chin.

'I used to be a farmer too,' Adil would begin and take a bite. Schlunk!

'I was stolen by the local pasha and brought over here.'

'I used to be a farmer *too*!' sighed Kemal and wiped a greasy mitt across *his* bristly chin. 'I raised sheep *too*.'

Their new comrade, swarthy, wordless, smelly Oddy, the Greek, would just lift his haunches and just made noise.

Pffffft-ffft-ffffffft.

'I used to raise sheep *too*,' started, gangly Gun. He used to be a farmer before he was hijacked and ended up in Gallipoli too.

The *heyamola* weren't as smelly as the Inglisz across the way in *their* fetid trench were though. The Inglisz could really use a bath and they were right next to an entire ocean too. All the *heyamola* could do is just pinch their nostrils ... or shoot them or something.

*A Sudden Finish*

Gallipoli finished rather suddenly.

At times it seemed like it would never end.

A lot of two-legged Arfstrayans copped a bullet. Most of them were shot by an enemy unlike the heroic four-legged

Arfstrayans who were shot by their mates. They'd been told by High Command that there wouldn't be any room for beasts on the ships home.

Simpson's Donkey was probably the bravest beast.

Its Simpson was a cockney migrant to Arfstraya. The donkey's job was carrying broken Arfstrayans down Shrapnel Gully. It really, truly was a brave beast. It tasted good too apparently. Oddy's tasty hot sandwiches were passed around the campfire with relish, literally and metaphorically too ...

Oddy's kebab sangers turned out to be much more successful than the bloody Gallipoli campaign itself was.

### Bloody Debacle

High Command finally decided Gallipoli was a disaster.

John-John's jingo-machine wouldn't admit it though. Gallipoli was even described as the place Arfstraya was born.

Listening to John-John's carry-on made it easy to forget that Arfstraya was on the losing side.

I think the modget was quite dangerous. He reckoned that young men in his day too should offer themselves up to another Gallipoli ... He wasn't talking about *his* kids of course. He was always cranking up the jingo-machine. He must have really enjoyed the pipsqueak sound of his own voice.

### The Traditions

The traditions all agreed on how Gallipoli *ended*.

They didn't talk much about how it began though. Turkey got invaded! Like I've already pointed out Gallipoli was so much not a glorious victory like the modget suggests. It was a glorious defeat!

## Another Lalor

One of Oddy's best mates in the Arfstrayan trench was a Lalor.

A Lalor had already figured in Oddy's life.

That was Lalor Senior the bully, Dad of the Junior who was one of Oddy's best mates at Gallipoli. Senior was always sniff-sniff-sniffing into his perfumed hanky everytime a riff-raff was about. He was a nob who led a revolt at the Eureka Stockade where Oddy found himself rather than just not be noticed. Shooting off Senior's arm was a mistake whatever tradition says Oddy did.

His descendant, Peter Lalor, the *not*-bully or Junior or Good Ole Egalitarian Pete or PL or Junior or Lieutenant Peter Lalor of the 12th Permanent Arfstrayan Force was Oddy's *best* mate and commanding officer at Gallipoli where Oddy was just Oddy The Foreigner. Everyone at Gallipoli was a *New* Arfstrayan ... except for the Turks.

## Old Social Distinctions

There were some things The First World War achieved.

*Some* old social distinctions were definitely broken down ... and it showed that everyone was basically the same *under the skin*. This was mostly demonstrated by ripping off lots of people's skins.

Lalor Junior would sometimes share a cigarette with Oddy on scary, moonless nights. Everybody's equal in Hades too.

## A Newe Worlde

Pete was committed to a newe worlde.

The Lalors re-made themselves when they came to Arfstraya and simply ignored a convict ancestor. Junior kept his plummy voice though. Oddy could just understand him.

Oddy had another trench-mate too, the murderous cannibal, William Edward Sing (Pte) or plain old Billy Sing who was a real arse-hole who out-ratted even the trench's rodents. Oddy had to listen to the slimy little rat's stories of murder and mayhem during his nocturnal travels morning after every tense early morning. He'd crawl back into their hole every morning as quiet as a ghost and cackle about all the scalping and gutting he'd just done. You can't tell a butcher off too much for butchery in an abattoir like Gallipoli though. He'd drop a souvenir gift from that night's trip into Oddy's fitful lap when he got back, a scalp, an eyelid or a lip and enjoy the screams. His best present to Oddy was some poor shade's full mustache once. Billy was considered a hero by newspapers back home though. He was named Spirit of No Man's Land. Gallipoli was a natural environment for the likes of Singo. He had lots of official approval. He was very good at doing whatever was expected of him. Authorities just loved him. He was awarded a DCM, a Croix de Guerre and lots of other gilt'n'ribbon from grateful nations. When Billy carked it years later though he did it in an anonymous boarding house. When he gurgled his last, he did it alone. When the shadow fell over Singo, it came as a relief.

### No Gods, No Masters
'No gods, no masters,' I hear the young people say down the pub sometimes.

### The Short Life Of Private Carver
Even Oddy got sick of Private Carver eventually.

A survival instinct insisted that a living person grow callous at Gallipoli.

There was a new breeze in the air. *Ancien regimes* were toppling all over the place, old monarchies, older aristocracies and imperial dynasties ... though not in Arfstraya. The British monarchy threatened to last even longer in Arfstraya than it would in the old Mother Country. Arfstraya was like some sort of teenager who didn't really want to leave home.

## The Charnel House

Oddy would need to get away sometimes and wander away from the charnel house down the beach next door.

The world was even coloured differently on the coast. It was purple and yellow with wildflowers down there rather than the cack-brown of the battlefield's rot, heat and dysentery. It smelled different and sounded different down there too. There was no tap-tap-tapping of rifles or crump-crump-crumping of shells. There were no flies buzzing. There was just surf shush-shush-shush-shushing like asking why-why-why. Even Bloody High Command could tell that the adventure at Gallipoli was over. The Boys could still be useful in France. The dream still dreamed on there.

## Joining Up

The two trenches grew closer and closer and eventually joined up.

The two mobs were close to getting rid of their armour and even started to stop mincing each other. A belief in absolute monarchy was growing weaker on both sides. Mortals were only human then too and so the closest the two sides actually came to joining up and being one was when a dog showed up one morning, some officer's poppet or pasha's toy, a running dog and lolloped between the lines, its tongue hanging out.

## Cries Of Horror

Cries of horror were common enough in Gallipoli.

Any cries of horror for the little bitzer were just lost in the hubbub. Heads poked up out of both trenches.

Standing up and showing yourself had never been too

advisable in kill-killer land. Running Dog kept pissing up and down the line and two sets of rifles stopped popping and grenade bombs from either trench stopped lobbing. The Dardanelles show was ending before peace broke out properly. A maddened bitzer puppy did what politicians had stopped even trying to do. It brought the two sides together in common purpose.

*Mince*

The pup was finally turned into mince when rifles did finally start popping again and everything went back to normal again.

Lee Enfields started squeezing again and Mausers squeezed back, bombs started lobbing and knives started knifing and soon it was there quite impossible to tell the difference between bloody man ribbons and bloody dog ones decking No Man's Land.

Digging with shovels and deepening trenches, sandbagging, standing up in a hole in the ground all day and night and just waiting soon permanently happening again.

*Deeper And Deeper*

One muddy, overcast day Oddy dug his trench deeper than he'd ever dug before.

Seamlessness existed only in perfect worlds like Olympus.

Oddy just dropped his rifle together with whatever it was that was still holding him together. He sagged against the side of his trench, dropped to his knees and started sobbing. Even High Whatever could see that Gallipoli was over now.

*Back Home*

Oddy found himself in a ship's bunk as narrow as a coffin back home.

Oddy was able to start dreaming again.

The Highest Command didn't really have anything to say to the hundreds of thousands of fodder who had already died.

*Mad Dogs And Flannels*

There's still one more Oddy-at-Gallipoli in Egypt story I should tell you.

It's a very Arfstrayan story ...

It's about a game of cricket.

A game was organised by the nobs to keep Arssie's competitive edge alive. They didn't want The Boys suffering withdrawal symptoms.

Nobs and gods are quite like each other actually. They both like organising mortals.

Anyway.

There was still some futile trench-life left in France as I might have already mentioned, so it was time to be enjoying flannels, tea and bashing of a leather cricket ball around instead of bashing each other up under that eternal eye of the desert Sphinx ...

What no one knew though was that there was an embittered anti-colonialist, anti-imperialist, anti-British, anti-everything, pro-Ottoman, mad tosser of a fanatical anarchist hiding inside the Sphinx in some crevice or other.

Oddy fielded ... and of all the survivors of Gallipoli playing that day, the dill had to go and pick Oddy to throw a bomb disguised as a cricket ball to. Oddy had always taken his games seriously so he was playing quite hard. He'd already caught two blokes out on the full ... so when he thought just another cricket ball flew at him on the full, he caught it and threw up into the sky in triumph just like the Boys around him did ...

## Bright Blue Skies

The skies were a bright blue that day.

The desert was a sparkling yellow and Oddy's bloomers a very loud white ...

This would've made a great colour photograph ... except that Oddy hadn't invented colour photography yet. He'd been away to war.

## Oddy Saved Lives

Oddy became one of those rare people at Gallipoli who actually *saved* lives.

He caught the ball on the full and threw it straight back up into the sky in triumph, a cricketing cliché he'd seen many comrades do before.

Oddy's ball exploded though.

An explosion in Gallipoli didn't raise too many eyebrows.

## Home

Oddy felt quite fed up at the end.

It's actually hard to know why Oddy even went back home to the lucky country. He must've felt that Arfstraya had always done things for him ... Okay. I'll just have to take his word for it. I would've thought that he was missing his latest *kyra*'s kisses maybe. They *did* taste just like wine apparently. He'd never found the black she shrouded herself in after her husband died somehow off-putting, however much harder to find she was after dark.

Oddy didn't leave her feather bed for days. He was very tired and slept a lot too. The only thing that got him out in the end was her singing ...

She'd already grown quite used to Oddy disappearing for a fair while when he played his cards and had his tiny coffees down the *kafeneion* so she had barely noticed him when he left for war instead.

### Yet Another Boarding House
Oddy left the *kyra* and their boarding house for another *kyra* eventually.

### The Bang And The Whimper
When Oddy left *kyra* Everithiki's the last morning, he felt a chill.

It *was* winter ... but this particular chill was because she'd read his coffee cup the night before and told him that there'd be another war one day even bigger than this one ... Even more men die or be maimed, so Oddy felt depressed and really needed to forget himself in some coffee and cards.

He just had to stalk out then. The front door banged behind him and frightened the little doggy in the front yard next door. It whimpered.

'That dog needs a good bone,' thought Oddy to himself.

When he left that *kyra*'s house for what he could see was the last time, he left without even a backward glance, the way he'd learnt was best, his eyes already turned to whatever was coming next. He already knew though that when something ended, something else was just beginning. Oddy just knew that his next *kyra* wasn't going to be any different to the last. She'd own her own house too and no longer have to rely on a bully of a husband.

In Arfstraya she could be her own person. Back home she was just a woman.

### What Oddy Wanted
Oddy never wanted much.

He just wanted Arfstraya to reward his service at Gallipoli with a stamp featuring *his* face ... He would've really liked his face quite close to a perpetual licking. A lick's not too different to a kiss as any talking dog can tell you. Having a face on a stamp is *like* getting a medal or official thank-you from a grateful nation.

Oddy would've been quite satisfied with just an *official* hot food vendor's licence for the big Anzac Day celebrations. Even the idea of a crowd made Oddy's mouth water.

## Phar Out

Only a bit's known about Oddy's later life.

He took one last big trip overseas. It was over water, his favourite thing. He travelled with his big brown mate, Phar Lap ... Phar was a horse.

## Throwing In The Apron

Oddy threw in his apron at this takeaway food shop he was working in at the time.

He'd had quite enough. He was working over the grill sizzling meat patties, bacon, onion, eggs, pineapple rings for the greasy hamburgers the place sold at a very decent profit. The owner was a cards crony of Oddy's. He'd do his bundle at the races every week and try to make his losses up cheating at cards. This so-called mate of Oddy's also didn't pay Oddy his fair wages. He even charged Oddy for sleeping in the storeroom out the back on a lonely single mattress with just one cold blanket. Oddy also got three hamburgers a day for breakfast, lunch and dinner. Oddy overheard other cronies down the *kafeneion* talking about a job as trainer *and* jockey for Phar Lap that was going ... Oddy had grown sick of his takeaway food job and he was getting on a bit now. Oddy loved the sport of kings and queens.

Oddy's latest best mate, Phar, Oddy knew also as PL was a horse with the heart of a lion. It was another one of those Arfstrayan heroes. PL was worth a lot of pounds, shillings and pence alive and a lot more to evil types dead. PL and Oddy hit it off straightaway and became best mates. PL had Oddy twisted around its hoof. Phar was no better at English than Oddy was.

The big brown lives in a glass display case now in a museum where people can look in on him whenever they want to. He's got no privacy. He can look out too if he wants to. Phar was stuffed with straw and he'd always hated the taste. He was a real Arfstrayan too. His mind was full of the idea of *race* which really got him going. What really grabbed Oddy was the idea of overseas travel with his mate.

## Oddy's Fault

Phar's death might have been Oddy's fault.

I think that maybe Phar bit off more than he could chew. Phar let him know that he'd had too much.

'Pfffaaaaaart!' he said odorously.

'Pffffffffffaaaart-pfffffft-pfffffffffft!' he said.

Horses don't always know when enough was enough. Phar blew himself up! Phar races around now in a pseudo-paddocks of asphodel by the River Styx, tossing and tossing his spectral head. Phar Lap was soon stuffed.

## Gertie

Oddy loved all his wives, whatever-her-name-was, Beryl and all his *kyries* too.

He loved them all in his way. The lady he dreamt about in his last bed in hospital was Gertrude Lowthian Bell or Gertie. Gertie was just perfect for Oddy. She was an explorer *and* a woman and she was already dead and where he'd be going too soon beginning with H. He at least got to meet the others. Oddy came across Gertie down his *kafeneion* … when the newspaper was read out aloud to him. There was an article in it about Gertie and their mutual friend, the desert.

Gertie could be seen as just an arrogantly stupid English woman. She wore just a light frock and carried a parasol as her camel plodded cross the sands. She was another Arfstrayan hero. The historical record forgets to mention the toasted *souvlaki* sanger with no camel that came in the mail. Gertie called her favourite camel Oddy. This could've been just a coincidence as she hadn't actually met ours yet.

It *could've* been a great love story. She claimed that *she* discovered Iraq which was called The Cradle of Civilisation or Wog-land, whatever the region's Arabic-speaking people knew it as. The Arabs were ruled by the Ottoman Turks back then, Oddy and Arfstraya's enemy at Gallipoli. The world's managed efficiently by Yankee super-imperialists now. Oddy's head shook and shook with dropsy or something when the bit about Gertie discovering Iraq in the paper was read out aloud down the *kafeneion*. He was really upset. Oddy knew that *he* was the one who discovered Iraq though, those Arabic-speaking people aside. He stumbled on the place on his slow way back from the Gallipoli campaign. Iraq was once only an administratively convenient cobbling together of warring desert tribes by some British imperialist. It took his usual bitter little cup of coffee and a dollop of *glyko* jam in a tiny glass dish with just one glass of Ithacan *raki* to calm him down so he could settle into his cards.

## Polka-Dots, Daisies, Yellow Submarines, Loud Wallpaper And Bad Trips

Close to the end of the story, Oddy got the best-paying job he ever had.

He went guru ...

This *was* the sixties, known also The Age of Polka-Dots,

Daisies, Yellow Submarines, Loud Wallpaper and Bad Trips ... or Artificial Stimulants or something ...

The ever-present promise of a trip was always attractive to him and so was the promise of making money for just answering some questions. Oddy described this job to Theo as the most un-menial one he ever had and ironically it paid more than all his previous jobs put together.

That was the type of time it was. If you didn't have a guru in those days it usually meant you were one.

### Being A Guru

Guru-ing was where the money really was.

Oddy even went to the trouble of learning enough English to answer questions at least. Oddy decided to set up shop in the city. He could sell a few *souvlaki* rolls in a slow, creaky way when a shaggy-haired young man in a torn striped muslin, see-through shirt appeared and asked for guidance.

Oddy offered him hot *or* cold takeaway food instead. They both seemed a bit non-plussed.

These were carefree, careless, cheap, money-less, self-serious times.

'What do I do now?' the young man wanted to know.

### White And Long

Oddy certainly *looked* wise now.

He wore his hair very long and white. Cutting it cost money so he just let it grow. Back at the city square gullible people who just wanted someone to talk about them a lot, self-obsession being quite usual at that time amongst hippies, lined up behind the young man and started firing questions at Oddy about the meaning of life and that sort of thing. People were willing to pay good money back then for *the truth*. Oddy saw that there was possibly good money in being a seer. That certainly involved less work than having to prepare takeaway food, hot or cold, and sell it. Oddy answered every question same way. 'Whatever you reckon,' he'd always say. Sharpies saw the really big bucks in a Whatever You Reckon cult with a long white-haired, white-bearded Oddy as seer ... Oddy bought the idea big. He wouldn't have to do very much for his money. The most energetic thing he had to do was rake in heaps of money. Oddy had always fed people. He just did that in a different way now. He answered all their questions. Oddy found *why* was the most popular one.

The answer was always *why not*. Oddy's Whatever You Reckon movement grew into a worldwide one.

He was finally being treated as the god on earth he was. Three simple words made Oddy richer than even he could have ever imagined. That confused muslin-shirted young man was just the first of many satisfied customers ... Oddy had just invented The New Age.

### Oddy's Confusion
Oddy's confusion just grew.

It's known nowadays as *stoned*.

### The Future
Oddy saw a few bob in this Guru business.

He started to look beatific and serene.

### Donations
Oddy had to get used to accepting donations.

People started just thrusting money at him for doing nothing except ... just being. The most energetic thing he had to do now was just accept people's devotion.

No, that's not quite true. He had to answer a few self-obsessed questions too. *Whatever You Reckon* was usually the answer ...

Questions were quite often clouded in a thick haze of aromatic smoke.

## Spliffs

Oddy's devotees would repeatedly leave something called ... *spliffs* instead of cash-money sometimes in the offerings-plate Oddy's sharpies would pass around.

*Whatever You Reckon* was becoming more and more of a real goldmine. Oddy found making money this way much much easier than having to stand over a grill all day ... especially now that he was getting on a bit. Oddy was living every migrant's dream. He was having money just about chucked at him. Oddy discovered later that working hard wasn't the only way of making a fortune in Arfstraya ... The sharpie disciples soon helped him found a chain of *Whatever You Reckon* commune/hotel/motel/shopping arcade complexes. Each one became known as something not too humble like the *Centre Of Meaning* ...

Humble Oddy could barely recognise what his life had become ... but he could barely recognise his own face in his own mirror on his own wall by then.

## Unbalanced Again

I lost my balance on the tram or train the other morning.

The oaf of a driver slammed on the brakes. Or he was taking the corner too fast or something.

A real tragedy almost came next. I was hugging two bottles of hops-juice to my chest and they smashed when I hit the floor. I was really looking forward to a few cool glasses of beer too ...

The days had been getting warm.

Gods have to catch trams too sometimes, you know. Flying's not necessary all the time, especially just over short distances ... I already had the shits. The doctor was carrying on at me again. She told me I was drinking too much, whatever that means.

### Another Stinking Hot Day
It was one of those stinking hot, crowded days on the tram.

I was hanging off my strap in the aisle ... This beautiful girl was sharing her cack-green tram seat with her main squeeze and she had a face on her like a cloud had just passed over the sun.

Her hair was a crimson mane. She reminded me of this tough, purple-haired goddess I used to know. Her hair was only dyed, I suppose. I'd forgotten that mortals could misunderstand. I leaned over and stroked it. I'd forgotten that my mortal disguise was old drunk. The goddess on the tram was really angry with her man ...

'Of course I *can* forget,' she ground her teeth.

We both held our breath.

'I'll *never* forgive you though!'

### I Don't Know
I'm not sure what he did.

I think I might have done it myself more than just once.

The driver slammed on his brakes then though, the big thumb, and I went flying! He must've missed the turn or something.

### Bloody Icarus
'Bloody Icarus,' I cursed after I thudded on the floor.

My bottles couldn't bounce though. I got upset and started stuttering and talk-talk-talking to myself. There was no law against crying back then either.

### The Gutless Wonder
The driver was so much not just a gutless wonder.

He had quite a big gut on him, tatts and a full head of greasy salt'n'pepper hair, combed back and brylcreemed and big sideburns. He didn't even pretend to care. This dark little guy with a downy mo on his lip leaned over and asked me if I was OK.

'Don't worry about the beer,' he said. He was obviously still too young to understand the significance of what had happened.

Mustafa or whatever his name was got me back up and into a seat ... and when I was settled he started screaming at the driver at the top of his lungs until the older bloke pulled over or whatever trams do and came down the aisle to see how I was. I'll never forget. It was the first time in my long life that I'd been apologised to by a man in uniform.

Thank the other gods for humans like the kind little guy.

I was shaking. That bunch of clucking, old white-haired, white-uniformed bowling ladies would just have to find someone else to stare at now. I had to get off the tram as soon as I could. I'd already missed my stop and yeah, no, I didn't get his name.

I'm not a cop.

*The Last Word*
Enough ...
That's got to be the last word. I'm thirsty now.